REAPER

RUTHLESS KINGS MC
BOOK ONE

K.L. SAVAGE

ISBN: 978-1-952500-00-8
LIBRARY OF CONGRESS CONTROL: 2020906026

PHOTOGRAPHY BY WANDER AGUIAR PHOTOGRAPHY
COVER MODEL:SONNY HENTY
COVER DESIGN: LORI JACKSON DESIGNS
EDITING: MASQUE OF THE RED PEN
FORMATTING: CHAMPAGNE BOOK DESIGN

FIRST EDITION PRINT 2020

To Wander and Andrey:

The people who put a face to the characters.

Wander, I have so much to say, but the words aren't enough. They say a picture is worth a thousand words, and my cover speaks volumes.

Andrey, your friendship and words of encouragement mean the world to me. You always go the extra mile for me, and it is something that never goes unnoticed. I swear you have superpowers.

PS: Donna and Wander joke around constantly; it's really funny to get to see and hear about. Well, one day while we were going back and forth getting the covers done, it started to be a running joke about who got to see the covers first, who's more special, lol. They both are special, some of the best people you will ever meet. But if I was going to pick a favorite, they'd tell you it was one of them, but they would be wrong.

Andrey wins every time.

There's no contest. Sorry not sorry ;).

CHAPTER ONE

Sarah

Six months after being rescued

NOTHING IS WORSE THAN WANTING SOMETHING YOU CAN'T HAVE. Mentally, I can. Emotionally? Eh, that's a dangerous line to tiptoe, but I'm dancing on it. Physically? No way in hell. It really sucks being seventeen and head over heels for the president of the Ruthless Kings. Reaper is everything I ever envisioned a man to be. Reaper, or Jesse, as I like to call him sometimes, which drives him crazy. I love to drive him crazy. The tic he gets in his jaw when he gets frustrated with me gets me all hot and bothered.

He is intelligent, brave, and kind. My most favorite thing about him? He is strong, and not because he is built with muscles and lean without fat, but strong in his mind, in his heart, in his soul. He carries the weight of the world on his shoulders, and no one even knows.

I do, though.

I see it.

I want to help him carry it all.

But I can't. I'm not eighteen yet, and he kicked me out of his room a few nights ago when I tried to make my move.

It was so embarrassing. Everyone watched me run to my room with tears running down my face, and my brother gave me a firm talking to. No one understands. I see the want in Reaper's eyes, the hard set of his lips as he looks at me as if he hates that he wants me. It's as if it hurts him to look at me.

And that only makes me want him more.

Every time he hops on his bike and leaves, my heart yearns, and the voice in the back of my head tells me he is going to go have sex with another woman because he can't have sex with me. The thought of him with someone else makes me want to take one of my brother's grenades and blow the bitch up.

I've thought about it.

I've thought about following him to see where he goes, whose pussy he is dipping into. I envision shoving him off her, fisting the grenade in her whorish cunt, pulling the clip, and watching the bitch explode.

Is it violent? Sure, but that's how he makes me feel. No one else is allowed to have him, and it takes all I have to hold myself back and not tell him point blank who he belongs to, but I don't. I sit back in the shadows and watch him.

Because if I do anything else, he calls me a kid in front of everyone.

I am young, but I've seen dark things that no one at any age should see. I might be young in age, but I'm old in spirit. I'm older than my years, and I hate that Reaper doesn't see it. He only sees the little girl who was beaten to a pulp, laying on the ground in front of his club. I'm wondering if that is all I'll ever be to him.

That damn voice in the back of my head tells me to move on, to forget about him, to find a man my age.

Yuck.

Boys my age are boring and soft. I want nothing to fucking do with them. They know nothing about life. Their main worry is getting to school and losing their virginity. They don't know the ways of the world. And their boyish looks do nothing for me.

No one compares to Reaper.

He towers with his massive height, and the hard edges of his face hypnotize me. His cheekbones, jaw, and nose are chiseled, and his flesh is tinted from the sun, making his eyes a bit paler because of the sunglasses he wears while riding his bike. On top of all that, he has thick hair that I want to tug and run my fingers through while I kiss his full lips.

His hair almost matches his eyes, and when those brown irises are set on me, my body trembles with excitement and just a pinch of fear. He is menacing.

And I want to be the woman that he comes home to take all that frustration out on.

He isn't violent. I don't have to worry about that. He is very careful with me, but I know the rage simmering behind those massive hands. And I know he and I can be good together, in and out of the bed, if he would give me the chance. That's all I want.

A chance.

"Hey, Sarah. Hellooo." My brother snaps his fingers in front of me, ruining my daydream of Reaper. Jenkins always finds a way to interrupt my thought process.

"What?" I snap and flip over in bed to give him my back. I'm not in the mood for visitors. I actually never am. The only person I ever want to see is Reaper.

"Come on. It's time to go to school."

"I don't want to go." He throws the covers off me, and the cold air hits my legs making me freeze. "Jenkins!"

"Whatever. Get the fuck up because we are leaving in five minutes. I let you sleep too long."

I groan as I get up. I really didn't plan on going to school today. A lot of the guys are going on a run, and Reaper is here alone with Poodle and Skirt. That means that the run that everyone else went on is dangerous, and they don't need Poodle and Skirt since they don't have murderous qualities about them.

Yet.

It's only a matter of time, but I think Poodle will break first because everyone gives him such a hard time about his dog.

Reaper being alone here means that I have another chance at talking to him and trying to win him over, so when I do turn eighteen, he won't question being with me; he'll just do it. We have a large age gap between us. He is in his prime at the ripe age of thirty-eight. Thirty-nine soon.

That's what makes him better than all the other boys my age. He has lived, truly lived. Reaper has experienced the ups and downs that life freely gives. I know he and I are meant to be together. We are cut from the same cloth.

Someone just waited to cut said cloth for a long time before making me.

I roll out of bed and smirk when an idea forms. I throw my hair up in a messy bun and rummage through my drawers. Drawers. A dresser. Something I've never had before, and

Reaper filled it to the max. He took me shopping and bought me anything I wanted.

And I am going to wear what he bought me. He is oblivious to what he got me all those months ago because everything was in a pile at checkout. I giggle when I pull out the black sheer off-the-shoulder shirt. Then I grab my black tank top and a pair of skinny jeans. That's when I notice my brother in the corner with his arms crossed, eyes shut, waiting for me.

"Can you go? I'm about to change."

He doesn't move.

"Jenkins!" I shout, and he nearly falls over, opening his eyes as he balances on one leg.

"What? What's wrong?" He scrubs his face.

"Did you fall asleep standing up?"

"No. I was resting my eyes. I'll be in the kitchen waiting for you."

Ah, the response a grandpa gives. Nice.

He shuts the door behind him, and I make quick work of my outfit. I throw my sleep shorts in the hamper along with my Ruthless Kings shirt. It's Reaper's. I wear it nearly every night. It makes me feel close to him.

I give myself one look over in the mirror and grin. A spray of perfume, deodorant, a few swipes of mascara, and then the final touch—cherry lip gloss. I know this will drive him mad because anytime I wear something that shows skin, Reaper gets this mad twinkle in his eye, and it really riles me up.

I grab my backpack off the floor and swing it over my shoulder and then take my helmet in hand. Ever since Jenkins got our father's bike when he turned eighteen, he drives it everywhere, even school and that means I ride on the back. Reaper wouldn't let me ride until I had a helmet, though, and of course it's bright neon purple. It clashes with the bike, and Jenkins can't stand it.

Reaper got me the helmet, so that means he has to care, right?

With a deep breath and butterflies in my stomach, I open the door and head out. Reaper is right there at the kitchen table, a plain white mug in his monstrous palm. It makes the fragile cup look so small, and then I imagine his hands roaming down my body, making me feel just as fragile and small, and goose bumps travel to a place that Reaper refuses to go.

His onyx eyes harden when he looks at me while he sips his coffee. "You aren't wearing that. Go change."

"Why? It complies with school regulations. Plus, we will be late if we don't leave now," I say with a shrug of my bare shoulder. His eyes drop to it for a split second, and his tongue flicks out to lick his lips before he hides them with the coffee mug again, schooling his face.

Am I imagining things?

"Don't care. Go change." His eyes never leave the inside of his cup.

"No," I say.

A sharp inhale of breath from my right makes me look at Jenkins, and he is shaking his head, hiding a grin under his hand.

"Sarah, get your ass back in your room and fucking change, right now!" Reaper's voice slowly starts to rise, and my body reacts to him in a way that I can't help. My young nipples bead with the authority in his voice.

I grab an apple from the middle of the table and throw it in the air, catching it so it doesn't land on the floor. "Hmm, let me think about it." I take a bite of the apple, and a bit of the juice dribbles down my lip. I wipe it off and suck my finger into my mouth, and Reaper's eyes never leave my lips.

At least, I think that is where his eyes are.

"No. I like this outfit. Ready, Jenkins?" I ask in a happy, chirpy voice. Poodle leans against the doorway and gives me a thumbs-up, telling me to stick to my guns.

"I swear to god I'll fucking burn that outfit when you aren't looking if you don't change," Reaper threatens.

"Then light it up, Jesse, because I'm going to fucking rock this outfit today. And if you burn it, I'll buy another." I lean down and give him a kiss on the cheek. Lowering my voice so no one can hear, I swallow my bits of apple and whisper into his ear, "I look forward to it, *Daddy.*"

A low growl rumbles his strong chest, and his fingers dig into his thighs until they're white from the pressure.

Mission accomplished.

I straighten and smile at Jenkins. "Ready, bro?"

He chuckles. "Yeah, kid. I'm ready. Let's go."

I make sure to sway my hips a bit as I leave, hoping Reaper's eyes are on me. Reaper doesn't have a conscience, until it comes to me. My father was his best friend, his club brother. He's sworn an oath not to touch me, but that doesn't mean I can't give him a show.

He better get ready because on the night of my eighteenth birthday?

The show is over.

CHAPTER TWO

Reaper

I T'S PROM SEASON.

I hate prom.

Everything about it. I didn't even go to my prom. I mean, I fucked my date for prom, but then I dropped her off at the school and rode off into the sunset by myself and came back to the club because no fucking way was I dancing in a damn stuffy suit and drinking punch that had no alcohol in it.

The reason why I hate it now has changed.

Sarah fucking Richards. The little maniac that came into my life like a damn tornado, completely messing up everything I thought I knew I wanted. She was trouble. A hot, off-limits, seventeen-years-old pile of damn trouble.

And she tempts me with it.

Like right now.

Prom is in three months, and she just *has to go* shopping for it. Her words. And, of course, none of her little girly friends can go. I'm not stupid. A woman like Sarah doesn't have chicks for friends. She has dudes. Sarah is rough around the edges, blunt, and when she wants something, she trudges headfirst and takes it.

Snatches it.

I have been in the snarls of her hands and let me say, Sarah has a firm grip. The relationship between us is strange at best. Her efforts of getting in my pants, yes, my pants, has failed.

For one reason only.

She's seventeen for another four months, and I swear I'm about to go out of my mind. I haven't even touched my cock since she came to live with us because anytime I do, my mind wanders to her, and I can't jack off to someone underage. I fucking won't. So I don't. I ignore my raging erections in the morning and at night, and any time I need them to deflate in a matter of seconds, I hang out with the cut-sluts.

I don't want any of them anymore. They don't drive me crazy and, apparently, I like crazy.

It's weird.

But I won't lie and say I'm not counting down the days.

And then I'll back out because I know that's the right thing to do. She's off-limits. Off-limits. Off-fucking-limits for so many reasons.

I've concluded I'm never going to have sex again because she is the only woman in my mind, and it's a problem.

"If I'm going, you two fuckers are coming with me." I point to my VP and Sergeant at Arms and then point to Boomer. "You too, kid. Don't you dare think you're getting out of this. If I'm going down, all of you are going down with me."

"But I'm busy," Tool pouts and stomps his foot. It looks ridiculous. He is an overgrown toddler. "I have ten oil changes, a radiator to replace, and a hundred tires to rotate today."

"Boo-fucking-hoo. Hand it off to Poodle or Skirt," I say, tucking my wallet in my back pocket. I look toward Sarah's bedroom and see the light on under the door. Her feet behind it causes shadows as she moves around, and I want to know what she is doing. What is she planning? Is she excited for prom? Who is her date?

I growl at the thought of a boy dancing with her at prom. I can dance.

When she's eighteen.

"Poodle barely knows how to put gas in his tank—"

"I resent that! I figured it out!" he hollered from the main room.

Tool rolled his eyes. "And Skirt, every time he bends over, I see the red hair on his ass, and it blinds me for like five hours."

"Aye, my arse is great to look at! Hair and all. Women love it," he grumbles as he grabs the apple pie from the fridge and stabs it with a fork, eating it right from the pan.

Tool lifts his lip in disgust. "Anyway, I don't want to leave my shop in their hands."

"Then I'll have Slingshot pull the slack," I say, kicking up my boots and laying them on the table as I lean back in the chair. I bend over and lick my thumb when I see some dirt on the front and rub it off. I may or may not have polished my boots for the trip to the mall, so Sarah isn't embarrassed to be around a bunch of filthy bikers.

But mostly because they look nicer. Yeah, that's the main reason.

"I'll do it!" he yells from the bathroom and then groans. "Sorry. I had leftover tacos for breakfast."

"Dude, TMI." Tool cringes, and Skirt continues to eat the pie like a fat kid at camp not bothered by gross things.

"Shut up, Slingshot." I raise my voice so he can hear me through the bathroom door. "Tool, Bullseye. You're coming. End of story."

"Fine, but I'm taking my flask."

"Me too," Bullseye finally speaks.

"I'll go," Tongue says out of nowhere.

"Shit!" Tool jumps.

"What the hell! Ah, look what ye made me do, Tongue. I dropped me damn pie on the ground!" Skirt groans, staring at the chunks of apples on the ground.

I chuckle. Tongue is a weird son-of-a-bitch. "Where are you, Tongue? Come out from your dreary corner and stop sharpening your blade."

A few seconds of silence and Tongue doesn't say a word. The guys are sharing glances, trying to prepare themselves for Tongue's random appearance. I'm starting to wonder if he is even in the room when a hand lands on my shoulder, causing me to nearly piss my fucking pants.

"I'm here."

"Jesus Christ, Tongue!" I yell. "You've been standing in the corner all this time watching us?"

"You all are very entertaining. So can I go to the mall? I find shopping relaxing."

I'm not going to ask. I don't want to know. "You can't sharpen your knives in public."

"Reaper," he whines.

I have never heard the man whine a day in his life. My boots

11

hit the floor with a solid thud, and I rub my eyes. I swear, being President is taking its toll. Most days, they're not grown ass men. They're children. "Tongue, you know what will happen if you whip a knife out."

"I promise not to stab or cut anyone. You know I always have to have my blade."

"Those are the rules of going prom dress shopping."

He stabs his knife into the table, right between my index finger and thumb. "Fine," he sneers. "But I won't like it." He thunders down the hallway and slams the door to his room.

"Jesus, he scares the hairs off me balls, I tell ye."

A snort escapes me at Skirt's comment.

Tool follows suit laughing.

Soon the entire room is up in loud bellows of laughter. I yank the blade from the table and fold it in. I stuff it in my front pocket, trying to ignore how many tongues have been cut with this knife, and do my best not to think about it. It's impossible, though.

"He is crazy," Bullseye says.

"Yeah, but he is loyal. Can't ask for better than that."

"Hell no. I want to see that man surrounded by dresses. That's going to be hilarious."

"Oh, I'm there."

"I want to go too."

"Me too!"

"Count me in. This ought to be good."

Before I know it, I nearly have half the club wanting to come with me prom dress shopping because they want to witness the scary Tongue around fluffy dresses and normal people. I'm not sure if I'm setting him up to fail or not. He isn't a circus, and that's how I feel like we are treating him. It's so rare that we see Tongue in public, so it's hard to say no.

I've only seen him out and about twice, and that was to get gas at the local gas station, and he went inside to get beer. Both times.

I've never seen him date. Never seen him with a cut-slut. He is a quiet person. When he has something to say, he means it. I know Tongue must really be unhappy if it means he can't bring his blade to the mall.

Toddlers.

Every single one of them.

"Okay, well. Get ready to go soon. Anything you want or need to get done, do it now," I say as I stand and stretch. "I'm going to check on Sarah to see if she is ready."

"Is she going to be okay with all of us going?"

"I'll ask, but I don't think she will care. She loves everyone the same."

"I don't know, Prez. I think she loves you most." Tool lays his hands flat and places them under his chin and then bats his eyelashes. "Oh, Reaper. You're the light of my life. I love you so." His voice is all high and pitchy, nothing like Sarah's at all which is smooth and raspy.

I yank the blade from my pants and toss it at Tool. It lands with a solid thud right next to his head against the wall, and he drops his hands. Everyone's smile leaves their face, and the fun atmosphere is gone. "Shut up. Don't make fun of her. She's a kid. Be better."

"She's like my sister. It's all in fun."

"It isn't fun. She doesn't love me. She's attached because of what brought her here. You heard Doc. She attached herself to me, not that you deserve a fucking answer. If she feels safe around me, then she feels safe. Don't ever make fun of her again; do I make myself clear?" I roar in his face.

"Yeah, Prez. I got it. I'm sorry."

That's when I notice I've gotten out of my chair, and I have Tool against the wall with the knife under his chin. I don't remember getting up. It's like I blacked out with pure rage. I let go of his cut and hit the knife against the wall. "Just don't let me hear it again."

"Yeah, Prez. No problem."

"I heard my blade?" Tongue says from the hallway. "I want it back."

I sigh, spreading my arm to the right and hold out the knife.

Tongue snatches it from me, and I watch as he kisses the sharp silver metal. "What did he do to you, huh? You okay?"

My brows raise when I witness him speaking to it as if it is a pet. The man is truly touched in the head. Good god, maybe he shouldn't come to the mall. I can only keep my eyes on so many of my brothers at once. It's like we are taking a damn field trip with how pissy they're all being today.

I take three strides, ignoring all the side glances I can feel at my back, and knock on Sarah's door. "You about ready? The dresses aren't going to try on themselves."

"Just putting on my shoes! I'll be out in a few minutes."

"Alright, d—" I catch myself before I call her 'doll'. It's been on the tip of my tongue for a year. She looks like one of those porcelain dolls; they're fragile but at the same time strong, just like Sarah. If I call her that, it means I have stepped over a line I cannot cross, and I'm barely standing on the right side of that damn line.

What kind of man am I that I've fallen to my knees over a seventeen-year-old-girl? I'm fucked in the head is what it is. This young woman has me wrapped around her finger, which no woman has ever been able to do. I need therapy for wanting someone twenty-something years my junior.

"If you aren't out in ten seconds, I'm not going," I shout through the closed door, feeling panic. I need to stay here. I need to hold down the fort.

The door opens, breezing her hair over her shoulders and wafting over her peach scent. She has no makeup on, and even natural she doesn't look so young. She looks like she is in her twenties with all that confidence radiating off her.

Fuck.

CHAPTER THREE

Sarah

I SMIRK WHEN I SEE REAPER'S FACE. HIS EYES ROAM MY BODY, eating up every inch of me. I know he wants me. I can see it in his eyes, and he is in for one hell of a ride if he thinks I'm going to ever back down. I won't back down until I get what I want.

Not only do I want Reaper, but I want his property patch. I'll keep fighting until I have it.

"Like what you see, Jesse?" I place my finger in the middle of his chest, and his strong heart beats against my finger. So sexy. His chest is so wide, I imagine myself laying across it, naked and sweaty. It will happen too. I just need to be patient.

His fingers wrap around my wrist, and I know I'm not imagining it because he presses against my hand for one split second before he throws my arm to the left and away from him. "Sarah, I told you not to call me that." The muscle in his jaw tics;

the sculpted bone is square and angry as he tries to scold me. It never works because I know what he really wants. "Can you manage to keep your shit together for more than five minutes?"

"Where's the fun in that?" I lean forward and play bite the air, just inches away from his lips.

"Fucking maniac," he grumbles as I walk by him, and Jenkins holds out my helmet.

I stop midstride and take a step back. "You have no idea, Jesse." I stretch out my arm and grab the helmet from Jenkins hand. "Who am I riding?"

Reaper punches the wall with his fist before turning around. "You aren't riding anyone. Stop talking like that."

"You going to make me?" I rub my slick lips together, and his eyes fall to my mouth. I make a show of it, flicking my tongue across my bottom lip, and the hint of cherry bursts across my tongue.

"Jesus Christ." He takes a cigarette from his pocket, places it between his lips, and lights it. I want to inhale the smoke he breaths out and bask in it. "Tongue, you deal with her. I'm not putting up with this shit today."

I stick out my bottom lip and pout. "You hurt my feelings, Jesse. You going to make it up to me?"

He takes a step forward, and a light amber glow swirls in his brown eyes. "When will you get it through your head that I want nothing to do with you?"

His words sting causing my heart to bleed, but I plaster on a flirtatious smile and meet his step with my own until I can smell the scent of rich leather from his cut, and a bit of the smoke lingering on his breath invades my lungs. Damn, he smells just how a man should. "Never, my skull's too thick to believe anything that comes out of your mouth."

"Can we go? This pissing match is getting old, and I want to get one of those buffalo chicken sandwiches from the mall. They always saturate it with hot sauce and ranch. It's so good." Poodle rubs his belly, and Knives nods in agreement.

"We can save this for later."

Reaper grabs ahold of my wrist again, and his eyes meet all the brothers in the kitchen before landing on me again. "Go outside. We will leave in two minutes. I need a word with Sarah."

Everyone starts to head out of the hallway, their big bodies lumbering behind one another in a single file line. The only one who doesn't move from his position is Jenkins— Boomer, these days after he killed the man who abused me. No one has told me directly about what happened, but word gets around in the club. It's easy to overhear things.

Everyone in the club has a dark side. Tongue cuts out tongues, but Jenkins' dark side is different. It's more vindictive. It worries me, but he protects me at all costs. Like right now, everyone else is outside, but he is propped up against the counter with his arms crossed, staring at Reaper with distrust and a bit of anger.

My brother tends to look like that most days. It's hard to tell if it is directed at everyone or if he really has it out for the club.

"You too, Boomer," Reaper states.

I meet my brother's gaze and smile. "I'll be okay, Jenkins. Really."

Once he hears my permission, he stares down Reaper before uncrossing his ankles and pushing off the cabinets with his boot. "I'll be right outside, Sarah."

Reaper tenses from the statement, and I understand why.

REAPER

Reaper has done nothing but be good to Jenkins ever since our father died. To not have Jenkins' trust, it hurts Reaper, and I hate to see him hurt. I'll have to talk to Jenkins.

Once we are alone, Reaper pushes me against the wall, and I moan, loving the bite of pain tingling my shoulders from the pressure from his hands.

"You have to stop doing this," he begs, desperation lacing his voice. "Sarah, stop. I don't want to have to take counter measures for your rebellion."

I arch my back, and my pelvis presses against his. I feel the plump flesh of his cock and grin. "Are you going to punish me?"

"Stop this!" he shouts, a bit of his spit flying, and instinctively I flinch. I know he'll never hurt me, but I can't help my body's natural reaction. "Have some respect for yourself, Sarah." He pushes off me, taking more of my heart with him. "We will never happen. You're too young. I wish you'd realize that. You are doing nothing for yourself but causing trouble."

"I could say the same for you."

"I'm not the one causing trouble," he says, taking a hit off his cigarette.

I chuckle softly and shake my head as I walk by him to get to the hallway. "No, I mean, one day you'll realize we are meant to be together, and we will happen, Reaper. You can count on it." I strut away from him, putting a sway in my hips. I feel his gaze on me, burning into my soul like it always does.

"You're fucking crazy, Sarah."

I run my hands down the walls as I continue down the hallway toward the front door. "I sure am, Reaper, and you love it." A smug smile teases my lips when I get outside and see the large group of men waiting to ride out. Reaper's boots pound against the floor behind me, and with each loud thud getting closer to me, the more mischievous I feel. Reaper's boots pound against the floor behind me.

For his sanity, I keep my mouth shut and dance down the steps; a playful tug of my lips makes my mouth twitch, and it takes all I have to hide it.

"You must have a death wish, girl," Tongue rasps, his voice long and slow with a thick Southern accent. It is obvious he isn't from here, but I'm curious where he is from. No one seems to know. I bet Reaper knows. He knows everything there is to know about the brothers of the club.

"It isn't death I'm wishing for, Tongue." I swing my leg over the back of the bike, preparing myself to 'ride bitch' as they say.

Tongue's back vibrates from his laughter, and his long hair tickles my nose when he turns to look at me over his shoulder. "You know he won't touch you, right? Not until you're eighteen."

Liquid heat pools between my legs from the words. The rumble of the motorcycle doesn't help either. I love the power sitting underneath me. There is something wildly dangerous about so much steel sitting there. "I know, but it doesn't mean I can't have fun torturing him until then."

"Can't say I didn't warn ya."

I pat Tongue's shoulder, the leather warm under my palm. The skull on the back of Tongue's cut stares at me while it wears its crown, underneath in red it says, "Ruthless Kings." The hollow black eyes of the skull sear into my soul, and I feel like one of them. I belong here.

REAPER

I shake my hair to get it out of my face and meet Reaper's eyes. He watches me as he mounts his bike, and he can't see it from where he is sitting, but my skin pebbles from his pissed off gaze.

Whatever. He wants me.

I slide the helmet on and wrap my arms around Tongue's firm torso. Tongue is hot, but too touched in the head for me. His abs flex under me, and I flatten my palm on his stomach, turn my cheek so it is laying on his back, and pretending I'm enjoying being so close to him.

"Listen, I don't have a death wish. You better stop that shit," Tongue drawls.

"I don't know what you are talking about," I reply with a grim hug, pressing my breasts against his back.

Reaper and I have a staring contest, but I see his displeasure, his anger, the jealous flare in his face. He pops his knuckles before he wraps his large hands around the handlebars. Well, if he wanted me to ride with him, all he had to do was tell me, and I would have proudly sat in the bitch seat behind him.

I blow him a kiss, and that jaw tics again as he revs his engine. The back tire fishtails as he slams on the gas, tossing up clouds of sand and gravel.

"Well, you've pissed him off," Tongue says as we pull out of the lot.

I don't bother answering since we are riding, and the wind and roar of motorcycles makes it impossible for him to hear me. I can't believe how many guys are coming dress shopping with me. It's a little ridiculous, and I know they aren't all going for me. I overheard them about wanting to see Tongue there and out of his element. I think it's mean that they want to look at him like some circus freak. Tongue is nice, weird, and borderline sociopathic I think, but what do I know?

He hasn't given me a reason not to like him or view him differently than all the other guys, so I won't view him like they do.

The sun is hot, and the air is dry in Nevada today. The heat sears my shoulders as it beats down on us. It feels good, and it has my eyelids feeling heavy. I want to nap, but I know I'd fall off this damn bike and break my neck.

A few of the guys pass us by, but Reaper stays next to me and Tongue. Every now and then he meets my gaze, and I wish so badly that my cheek was pressed against his back. I act like his rejection doesn't bother me, but I'm heartbroken on the inside. I cry almost every day, hating that he fights me so hard. Part of me wonders if when I turn eighteen, if it will even matter.

He always rides next to whoever I am riding with, but he never lets me ride with him. I turn my head away from him, tears springing to my eyes as I look over the desert, seeing dried plants and tall cactuses along the small hills. I often wonder how many bodies are buried out there, in the vast and almost never-ending land of sand. It may be a weird thought but being around all these bikers who do illegal things, it's hard for the mind not to go dark every now and then. How many bodies has Reaper ordered to be tossed out there for the crows and vultures to eat?

One day, I'd like to take a little adventure through the desert and see just how many bones I can find. Me and Reaper, alone in a tent and building a fire to stay warm? Especially when the nights get so cold...

He'd warm me up, that much I know.

REAPER

If Reaper doesn't take my heart, then it will be broken forever, and I'll end up just as old and dry as the tumbleweeds that roll across the road.

Forgotten and alone.

I've been there once, and the thought of being there again, well, I'd rather die than to experience that again.

CHAPTER FOUR

Reaper

I AM OUT OF MY ELEMENT HERE, AND SO ARE THE REST OF THE GUYS. Here we are, a bunch of bikers, a rough looking crowd wearing leather cuts, and we are sitting on pink velvet couches in front of the dressing room.

I've never needed or wanted a cigarette so much in my life.

"Look at Tongue helping out Sarah. I think he likes it here." Knives points to our right, and all the men turn their heads to see Tongue and Sarah at one of the silver racks. It's comical because Sarah is so small and Tongue is huge, towering over her as he lifts dresses in the air and against Sarah's body.

Mothers are keeping their daughters a bit closer or outright leaving. We have this place to ourselves. I sigh with impatience as I wait for Tongue and Sarah to come to the dressing room. Her arms are filled, and he is carrying dresses too. There must be fifty dresses between them.

Fuck, this is going to take forever.

"Tongue looks like he is in his element, while at the same time, out of his element because he seems so knowledgeable, but how does he know about fashion?"

"No idea, Tool. There seems to be a lot about him we don't know."

After an hour browsing the damn racks for every single dress, they make their way back and Tongue is carrying most of the stuff. I can't help but smile when I see how ridiculous he looks. Shit, how ridiculous all of us look. He is over six-feet-four carrying slender dresses, and we are dressed in mostly black, sitting on pink fucking velvet.

When did this become my life?

"Alright, are you ready?" Tongue hangs the dresses up in the fitting room in front of us, and Sarah wraps her arms around her waist, looking a bit unsure or insecure. I can't put my finger on it exactly, but she looks her age right now.

We need to hype her up. I bet she feels like we don't want to be here. Tongue takes a seat next to me and rubs his hands over the soft material of the couch. Since it is velvet, every time his hands glide over the material it looks shiny and then dull. "Oh, this is nice. We need one of these for the clubhouse," he admires.

"Can you imagine cleaning the cum stains off this?" Tool gripes.

Sarah's cheeks tint with a light pink blush when she overhears Tool's foul mouth. I slap his chest, and the loud thud makes the snickers and immature chuckles die down. "Shut the hell up. We have a lady present. Apologize to her," I demand.

"I apologize, Sarah." Tool bows his head, and Slingshot slaps the back of Tool's head, calling him an idiot.

"You going to give us all a show, so you know what we

think about the dresses?" Jenkins asks, sitting on the arm of the couch at the very end.

She rubs her hands together and toes the ground, not meeting my eyes or looking at any of us actually. I've never seen her so out of her element. "I don't want to make you guys wait. I know all of you don't want to be here. It's okay."

"What?"

"No way!"

"Of course, we are interested!"

"We have to approve it. Why do you think we are here?"

"That's just nonsense. We are excited for the runway show. I expect twirls and spins and poses. I'll get my camera out." Poodle digs into his pockets for his phone. "Shit, where is it?"

All my guys are coming through like champs. They know they need to, or I'll fucking kill them.

"Left back pocket, ye shite," Skirt grumbles, and his voice scares the shit out of me. I had no idea he was even here.

"You better try on every single dress," I say, and all the men agree, nodding and mumbling, "Hell yeah." The biggest smile graces her face and, damn it, if my heart doesn't melt to see her that happy. That's all she needs to feel confident again and not like a burden. I hope she never feels that way.

"Okay," she squeals, and the loud pitch makes me wince. Damn, she sounds like a teenage girl now, that's for damn sure. "You guys have to be honest," she points to all of us with her index finger.

"Have ye met me?" Skirt chimes.

"Honesty is the best policy," Tool says next.

"I swear it on Lady's life." Poodle crosses his heart.

"Promise, sis." Jenkins holds up his hands like he is surrendering, and everyone that didn't say anything agrees.

She claps her hands and does a little dance, looking so damn cute. I want to pick her up and swing her around and celebrate her joy, but I can't. I never can. I can only support her happiness, and if that means spending all damn day at the mall while she tries on dresses, then that's what it fucking means.

"Okay, give me a few minutes." She turns around and vanishes behind the pink curtain, sliding it shut so nothing can be seen. A few women go into the other dressing rooms, and some are giving us the look of invitation, especially the brunette at the end. She's staring at Tool hard enough; he just might burst into flames.

"Don't mind if I do." He goes to stand, and I grab his cut and yank him back down.

"Don't even fucking think about it," I growl, making sure he hears the warning in my tone. "You aren't disappointing Sarah over some pussy. You hear?"

"Yes, Prez," he relinquishes, slouching against the couch.

Fucking headaches. Every last one of them.

The lights above us shine against the curtain just right, showing a faint glimpse of Sarah's shadow behind the veil. The outline of her body shows, giving me a slight tease of what she has been throwing at me.

What I've been fucking dreaming about. Christ and now I see the shadows of her small tits and perk roundness of her ass. My cock plumps, and I have to look away.

Only to see all the guys staring.

"Eyes fucking off!" I slap the back of Tool's head just like Slingshot did.

"What the hell? Why am I getting hit on the back of the head?" Tools rubs the spot that's getting abused, and I turn to Tongue to slap him, but he has a knife out, picking at his nails.

"Tongue..." I pinch the bridge of my nose with frustration. "I told you not to bring a knife to the mall."

He holds out the blade and scoffs, "This isn't a blade. It's a Swiss Army knife. I'd hardly even call it a weapon."

"Tongue, put it away."

"I'm never allowed to do anything," he pouts, and the sharp swift of the blade cutting through the air makes a mother and her small daughter scurry away faster as Tongue tucks it back in his pocket.

"You're going to get us kicked out of here, and she will be really upset. You fuckers can hold it together for a few hours."

Most of them mumble in agreement, and I cross my arms, waiting for Sarah to come out with the first dress. I never take my eyes off the shadow of her body again. It's like watching a peepshow, only to never have the veil uncovered to reveal a naked body.

Best friend's daughter. Best friend's daughter. Too young. I chant my new mantra. I might as well get it tattooed on me. I say it when I wake up, throughout the day, and before I go to sleep. Let's not forget all the times I wake up in a puddle of my own cum.

If she's so forbidden, then why am I keeping an internal clock of the day she turns eighteen?

"Are you ready?" she shouts from behind the curtain.

A roar of cheers and claps sound to tell her we are, and when the curtains slide open to reveal the woman who drives me crazy, my heart stops. I can't catch my breath. She's stunning. In this moment, she isn't Hawk's daughter; she's the sole desire of my attention.

"Wow," the men say in unison, staring her slack-jawed and stunned.

I want to gouge their eyes out for looking at her, for

seeing her look so classy, and for seeing the curves of her body that are meant for me.

Fuck, I don't mean to say that, but the dark part of me knows it is true.

"I don't like it," Tongue chimes in, ruining the moment of silence we all took to appreciate her beauty.

This time, I do slap him. "What the fuck? What's wrong with it? She looks beautiful."

"You think I look beautiful?" She takes a step forward, grabbing the sides of the light bronze gown so she doesn't trip over it.

Fuck, she's going to run with this compliment and torture me more. If I lie, it will only hurt her.

"The color is all wrong for her skin tone." Tongue stands up and rubs his fingers on his chin, then he strokes his beard as he analyzes the dress like some sort of expert. "The halter top"—he sighs—"I'm just not sure about it."

"Yeah, I thought so too," she says. "It makes me feel—"

"Like a child?" he finishes for her. I sit back, eyes wide, and I know the other men look the same because no way in fucking hell is this Tongue, the guy who makes it impossible for people to speak, the same guy who lurks in corners, the same guy who hardly speaks a word.

How is this the same man?

"Yes," she agrees.

"Go change and throw this over. I'll go put it back."

There's that smile again. "Thank you, Tongue!" She jumps up and gives him a kiss on the cheek.

My fingers rub against my jeans as my fists clench. Those are my kisses, but I can't do anything about it. I can't claim those kisses yet.

A few minutes later, the dress is tossed over the top of the dressing room, and her beautiful body is on display again. Her shadows dance like an erotic movie, and I watch every single scene, so I don't miss a thing.

"Ready?"

The sound of her voice brings me back to reality, and she steps out in a dark emerald green dress. It's low cut, too low cut. It shows too much of her tits, and it clings tightly to her body. I march my way toward her and push her back in the room. "You aren't wearing that."

"I thought it looked great."

I point toward Tongue, trying my best for my finger to look threatening. "Shut it."

"You didn't like it?"

"No," I growl. Of course, I didn't. It showed too much of what was mine. I want to buy it so when she is old enough, she can wear it for me. Then I can bend her over, lift the dress, and fuck her. I'll come all over the gown, staining it, and ruining it so it can never be worn again. "Fuck!" I shout, rubbing my hands over my face. "Just change."

"Okay," she whispers, and her big brown eyes well with water as she looks away. She looks so dejected.

I place my finger under her chin and lift her face to look at me. "It isn't because you don't look stunning. You could wear a trash bag and make it look good. For once, don't question me; just know I don't want you wearing that dress."

"Okay, Jesse."

For once in her life she doesn't argue with me, and I consider it a win. I take a deep breath and flop onto the couch, wishing it would swallow me whole.

The next dress is the same as the last, and when I look at my watch, two hours have gone by. It isn't because of the dresses not being perfect; it's because I've said no to every single fucking one. She looks too beautiful, too innocent, too touch worthy, and I know those teenage assholes are going to try to get with her at the prom.

I've been a teenage boy. I know what they want.

And it isn't to have a picnic at the park. We might say that to sweep you off your feet, but you better believe we are going to try to sweep you onto your back and fuck you if we have the chance. And honestly, boys grow into men, but we don't change that much.

"It's the last dress, and I really like it, okay? Keep that in mind when I come out," she says from behind the curtain.

A faint snore comes from my side, and Tool has fallen asleep. I elbow him hard in the ribs, and he jolts forward, whipping out his screwdriver so fast it's nothing but a blur. "What? Stay back! I'll fuck you up, bitch."

"What? What did I do?" Sarah asks, her fingers curling around the curtain. She sounds scared.

"Not you, doll," I reassure her and slap Tool's head again. "Get your shit together and put your Philip's head away. We aren't at war."

"Sorry, Prez. Bad dream."

"You were only asleep for two minutes."

"That's all it takes, Prez," Tongue says slowly in his Southern accent. The damn knife is back out.

Fuck it. He can keep the damn thing out.

"We are ready for you, Sarah." I lower my voice so only the men can hear it. "She likes this one, so get your head in the game. I swear to god, you assholes can't do anything a woman asks you to do, and it's sad. All of you will be rotating duties at the clubhouse, and we will be talking about this in church."

The glide of the metal rings against the rod tell me she has opened the curtain. Everyone is looking at her but me because I have to keep these nitwits in line.

"Wow," Poodle says.

I finally give Sarah my attention, and my world comes to a complete halt. Why does she have to be seventeen? Jesus Christ. I've never wanted a woman so bad in my life. She looks like something out of a fairy tale. The dress is a soft yellow, strapless, and the bodice is tight, but the body half is flowy with that fluffy shit that girls love. Sarah gives us a spin, and I know she feels beautiful because of the smile on her face.

Jenkins pushes off the couch and pulls Sarah in for a hug, kissing her temple. "You are beautiful."

"Thank you."

All the guys shout and cheer, bringing their fingers to their mouth and whistle. I can hardly move. I want to whisk her away and never look back. I shouldn't be thinking about this, but I'm jealous over some kid who gets to take her to prom and dance with her. He will have his hands on her, and I have never hated our age difference so much in my entire life.

I can't let her go to prom unsupervised. I'll have to talk to the principal. Don't dances need chaperones? I'll have to look into that. That will give me the opportunity to be there and lurk.

"Do you like it?" she asks me, and I know if I ruin this for her by not saying she isn't perfect, I'll ruin this dress and prom for her, and I can't take that away.

"You look like you stepped off the runaway, doll," I say, letting the nickname I have for her slip. She's my doll.

"Thank you for bringing me."

"Do you need anything else? Shoes? Jewelry? What do women need for this?"

"I don't want to impose or anything," She runs her palms down the front of her dress. "I can look at the shoes and jewelry here."

I scoff. No woman who belongs to Ruthless will wear fake shit. "No, doll. We will get you everything you need."

"Can we get food first? I'm about to die," Poodle asks, rubbing his stomach, and Sarah nods and laughs. I hope like hell he took pictures of her in every single dress because I want to look at them, frame them, and always have them on me.

Sarah turns around and walks away, and the small, lean lines of her shoulders show elegantly. I want nothing more than to feel how soft her skin is. Sarah is going to be my ruin with how she tests my patience.

Hell, she is my ruin.

CHAPTER FIVE

Sarah

BY THE TIME WE GET HOME, I DON'T JUST HAVE MY PROM DRESS, but ten other bags full of clothes. Everyone wanted to buy me something at the mall. They spoiled me. I have new outfits, new shoes, a new hair straightener, makeup; everything a girl could ever want—these guys got it for me today.

The best part of the day was when I walked out in the yellow dress and Reaper looked at me as if I was the only woman in the world. That's how I always want him to look at me. He has no idea how special of a man he is, and having his attention on me today, nearly all day, is something I will always remember.

I don't look at him like a father figure like most people think I should. I never have because I've never seen the age difference between us. I only notice the feeling I get when I'm around him.

This soul-pulling need to be in his arms and surrounded by him is an emotion that consumes me. I can blame it on the age, on my youth, but I won't because I've seen and experienced things people never do in their entire lives.

I'm seventeen, but I've seen plenty of life for the rest of my life.

All the engines shut off one by one, leaving the night quiet. It's odd not hearing the roar and feeling the vibration under me. Crickets sing, and every so often the glow of lightning bugs light up the sky along with the stars. I love it here. It's so peaceful. I know there's a darker part of the club they keep from me because I've experienced so much darkness myself. They won't be able to keep it from me forever, but for now, I'm going to soak it up.

"What's on your mind, sis?" Boomer, I need to get used to calling him that. My brother isn't patched into the club yet, but after what he did to my abuser, he earned his nickname. I love him so much for taking that nightmare away from me.

Tongue grabs my bags and kisses my cheek. "I'll set these in your room. I'll see you later."

"Thanks for everything. You were a really great friend today."

No one must tell him that because he grins, and he never grins. I had no idea he had such nice teeth. Happiness looks good on the brooding man. "It's what I'm here for." He makes his way up the steps along with everyone else. Reaper hangs out on the porch with Tool as they smoke, never taking his eyes off me.

I cross my arms to keep myself shielded from the cold air and sit on one of the tree stumps they put in the ground last summer for extra seating when they have their gatherings.

Boomer takes a cigarette out, and as the match glows in the dark, illuminating his face, all I see is Dad.

He looks so much like him it's scary, and it makes me miss what I never had even more.

"Looks like you have the guys wrapped around your finger, especially Tongue. I'm not surprised. You're the best." He throws his arm around my shoulders, and I lay my head against him, sighing in content.

How can this be my life now when a year ago I was fighting just to survive another day?

"I love you, Jenkins." We never say it enough, and I want him to know.

"I love you too, sis."

I love that he never hesitates to tell me when I say it to him. "You know, this life, it doesn't have to be yours. You can be more than this. You were made for more."

"There's nothing wrong with this life." I feel like I've been slapped. The club is everything. They saved my life. I owe them. "What's been your deal lately? You act like you hate it here."

He lifts a shoulder, blowing smoke out into the cold air. "I'm just saying. You can be more. I'll have your back, no matter what. We can leave, we can do whatever you want."

"You'd do that for me?"

"You're my family, my blood; I'd do everything for you, Sarah."

"Do you not think the club would? They have been nothing but kind to us. We don't need to have this conversation again, Jenkins."

"They're the reason Dad is dead."

"They're the reason I'm alive," I counter and huff, quickly standing to my feet. I need to get away from his sour mood. I love my brother, but I can only handle his bad attitude in small doses.

"Sarah—"

A loud *bang* ricochets against the air, interrupting the peaceful silence, and I watch my brother fall to the ground, blood staining his shirt. "Jenkins!" I go to run to him, but another shot rings through the air, hitting the dirt next to my feet. "Jenkins!" I scream at the top of my lungs, watching the bloodstain spread across his chest. Tears fall to my cheeks, and I'm tackled to the ground, the breath whooshing from my lungs from the hard hit.

"Shh, doll. Stay on the ground. I got you."

"Jenkins," I cry out again. "Jesse, he was shot. He needs help."

"I know, but the guys are spreading out now to find out who did this. I need you to stay down on the ground while I go check on Jenkins, okay? Can you do that for me?"

My body trembles violently, and Reaper's fingers graze my knuckles. "Sarah, can you do that?" he asks again.

I nod, digging my chin into the dirt, and salty tears run down my lips. "Ye—yeah," I stutter. "I can do that."

"Good girl." He kisses my forehead for a few seconds longer than what is necessary, and I hold onto his cut for dear life.

"I don't want you to go," I whimper. I'm scared. What if he gets shot?

"I'll be okay. I promise." He rolls off me, and his weight his instantly missed. Reaper army crawls to where my brother lays, unmoving.

And I just know he is dead.

Dirt embeds itself under my nails as I grip the ground for dear life. This isn't fair. It isn't fair for me to survive what I did, meet my only family, and then not even a year later have my brother taken from me.

"Boomer." Reaper flips my brother over, getting his face from the ground. "Boomer, talk to me. You're going to be fine, okay? You're going to be just fine." The hysteria in Reaper's voice lets me know that everything may not be fine.

A few more rounds of gunshots ring through the air, and I cover my head and cry. "Oh, god!" I'm not sure how long the gunfire goes on for. It feels like hours. My body has made itself home in the sand and gravel. My elbows sting for some reason, but I don't need to worry about that right now.

I lift my head to look at Reaper and Boomer, and Reaper is pressing against the wound on my brother's stomach to staunch the bleeding. It's dark, making it difficult to see, but I notice his hands are coated in something.

And I know it isn't dirt.

Silence falls again.

The crickets don't sing like they did moments before. They're scared, just like the rest of us. My ears ring, and when I hear footsteps getting closer to me, all I see are boots. Everything slows down. I can't breathe. I kick and fight whoever has ahold of me, refusing to go anywhere. I need to get to my brother.

"Sarah! Sarah, it's me. It's Tongue. I got you. You're safe. You're safe." He holds my hands behind my back, controlling my movements so I don't hit him in the face, and I finally snap out of it.

Tool, Slingshot, Bullseye, Pirate, Ghost, and all the other brothers walk from over the hill, everyone carrying guns. The moonlight shines from the handles and silver barrels, and Bullseye's is still smoking, swirling in the air.

"Update me," Doc says as he flies out of the house, half-asleep with bags under his eyes. He just pulled a forty-eight-hour shift at the hospital and had only gotten about an hour of shut eye before all this happened. Reaper ordered him to never put himself in harm's way because the last thing we needed was something to happen to our only doctor.

"He has a gunshot wound to the abdomen. There's a lot of blood, Eric," Reaper exclaims, never taking his hand off Boomer's stomach.

I forgot Doc has an actual name. It isn't often that I hear it.

Eric slides to their sides, runs a hand through his hair, and curses. "Fuck, okay. Take him downstairs. He needs surgery. I have everything I need here."

"Tool, Slingshot, carry Boomer to Doc's operating room. Now, and fucking hurry." Reaper doesn't move his hands until last minute, not until Tool and Slingshot have Boomer in their arms.

"He will need blood."

"I'll donate," I said quickly. "We are the same blood type."

"I'll need more than you can give. What type are you?"

"A negative." Any hope I felt at all deflated.

"I'll donate too. I'm O negative."

"Round up anyone else who can donate, Reaper. With you guys never going to the hospital, I need to keep a stash here." Doc gives me a saddened look and squeezes my arm before he runs up the steps and into the house to operate on my brother.

Reaper shucks his shirt off and wipes his hands on it. "Any news? Who was it?"

"We don't know." Ghost sighs. "One of us shot him. We followed the blood trail, but it was too damn dark. We will need to wait until morning. There's no way the guy survived. Too much blood."

"Get a fucking flashlight and go search that desert before the damn birds get to it. I don't give a fuck if it takes all night. Go!"

"Yes, Prez. Let's go boys!" Bullseye whistles and rounds up all the brothers, everyone except Tongue, who still has ahold of my arms.

There is no hesitation in Bullseye's voice. He does what the President says, no questions asked. All of them run to the shed on the side of the clubhouse and a few minutes later, the night is pierced with light. At least ten guys disappear beyond the ridge, and I'm scared for every last one of them.

"Sarah?" Reaper walks to me slowly like I'm a scared animal. "Are you okay?"

Am I okay? No, no, I'm not fucking okay. I just witnessed my brother getting shot, possibly dying. Where in the fuck does that make me okay? I don't make eye contact with anyone, not even Reaper, and keep my gaze on the ground. I try to tug free of Tongue's grip, but he holds firm.

"You can let me go. I won't break. I didn't before, and I won't now," I say the words with slight irritation as I rip my arms from him. I hate that everyone sees me as this weakling because I'm a woman. I can handle myself.

"I don't think you would. I just want to make sure you're okay," Tongue states, pushing a piece of my hair out of my face. It's a sweet gesture, something so opposite of who he seems to be.

"Go with the rest of them, Tongue. I got this." Reaper steps in front of me, something a possessive boyfriend would do, and Tongue peers around the big frame blocking me and nods. His boots crunching against the small rocks get further and further away until I can no longer hear them. He is too far away for me to know if he is okay.

REAPER

Reaper slides his hands up my arms, spinning me around until I'm locked in his worried gaze. When I see the warmth of his brown eyes, my heart stops racing, and my head begins to swim from the adrenaline crashing. "Are you okay, doll?" Reaper guides me toward the house, but I plant my feet, not wanting to take another step closer.

"I can't be in there right now, not while... I just can't." I fold my arms in on myself and sit on the stump again. "Oh!" I fall back when I see the muddy dirt mixed with blood, and Reaper catches me with his arms.

"I'd rather us be inside. I don't know who is out here, and I don't want you to get hurt."

My eyes are so raw and swollen, and that's when I realize I haven't stopped crying. "Will he be okay?" I ask through a scrambled voice choked with emotion. "Nothing can happen to him, Reaper. He's my brother. I need him."

"I know you do, doll. It's okay. He is Hawk's boy. It's going to take more than a bullet wound to get Boomer down."

My legs are weak, and I stumble over my own two feet. Reaper catches me again, but this time he swings me up into his arms and carries me up the steps. I let him. My body feels so heavy right now. I lay my head on his shoulder and let the tears come as I think about my brother. I don't think I'll ever get the image of him falling limp to the ground with blood pooling around him out of my head for the rest of my life.

Reaper pushes the saloon doors open, and the scent of the clubhouse comforts me. It smells like leather and smoke, something that shouldn't feel so cozy, but it does. Reaper sits on the couch, never moving me off his lap as he runs his fingers through my hair. His cheek lays on the top of my head, and I wrap my hands around his neck, burying my nose in the crook of his neck, inhaling the warmth and the lingering smell of Irish Spring soap from his skin.

On any other day, I'd try to rock against him to see if I could get a reaction out of him, but not today. I want to be held right now.

"I'm scared, Jesse."

"No matter what, you have me, okay? You have this club. You won't ever be alone."

I cry until his bare shoulder is wet, and my eyes shut for the final time through the night. Hopefully, when I wake up, this will all be a really bad dream.

CHAPTER SIX

Reaper

I'M NOT SURE HOW LONG WE SAT ON THE COUCH UNTIL I REALIZED she fell asleep. I close my eyes and hold her closer. Her heartbeat drums against my chest, steady and strong, just like her. No one else is around, no one else can see me enjoying this moment more than I should, but no one knows how hard it is to go through every single fucking day unable to fully take a breath because I can't touch her.

So I'll take this.

I'll hold her all night and comfort her. It's innocent looking, but internally, it gives me some form of relief. I'm able to take a deep breath for the first time since she stumbled into this clubhouse, all battered and bruised, making me weak in the knees from one look. This woman has me wrapped around her fucking finger.

I run my fingers through her sun-silk strands. They're so soft, softer than I thought they would be. Burying my nose, I close my eyes when I smell peaches. Fuck, I love her scent. It calls to me in ways I haven't been able to understand. It's like I've imprinted on her, like an animal would.

She deserves better than some old biker. I dream of the day she turns eighteen, but what then? She's going to be forty, and I'm going to be sixty-one? What life is that for her? I'm nearly past the prime of having kids. I've lived my life, and she has just started. It would be selfish of me to take the good years ahead of her.

And I want to be. Fuck, do I fucking want to be selfish with her, but I know my little maniac deserves better. Maybe she can find someone just as crazy as her. The thought of another man with her … it makes me see red. I want to kill anyone who stops me from having a life with her.

"Reaper?"

Shit.

I clear my throat and lift Sarah off me to lay her on the couch. I feel like I've been caught doing something I'm not supposed to be doing. Sarah tightens her hold around my neck and whimpers into my shoulder.

"It's fine," Tool says as he sits on the couch beside us. "Don't wake her. I'm sure she feels safe right now."

I swallow, knowing there is an unspoken understanding and question in the air between us. I think I like to pretend everyone has no idea about whatever is between Sarah and me. It makes it easier to handle.

Tool has blood on his hands and a smear on his neck and cheek. He looks exhausted.

"How long has it been?" I whisper the best I can as to not wake Sarah, but my voice still booms. She sighs against me, and the puff of her breath is hot on the side of my neck. Goose bumps arise all over my body, and I curse myself for reacting the way I do.

"A few hours. Doc is still working. Slingshot is helping him. It's not good, Reaper. Both me and Slingshot donated, but you're going to have to go down there to give more. The guys need to get together too. We need all we can. Doc can't stop the bleeding."

"Just give me a minute, okay? Let me take her to her room, and we can talk about this. I don't want her overhearing anything." To be honest, the last thing I want to do is take her to her room. Having her in my arms feels so good, and I know I won't get this chance again for a while.

Knowing she is devastated about her brother makes me hold my shit together. The last thing she needs to see is me falling apart. I'm the backbone of the club; people look up to me for guidance and strength. On the inside, I'm screaming at the top of my lungs, ready to go on a murderous rage. If anything happens to Boomer, I'm going to tear this fucking city to the ground to find answers, and if Boomer dies, there won't be enough men to contain my wrath.

That kid is the son I never had. When Hawk left me in charge of him, I had convinced myself there was no way I could do it. I knew nothing about kids. I managed to get him this far without getting injured, and now he is fighting for his life.

Sometimes I wonder if I do more harm than good, especially since the kid has a big fucking chip on his shoulder. The older he gets, the more I think he hates me. He has every right to if I think about it. His father is dead because of the club, he might die because of the club, and I'm pretty sure he knows about how Sarah feels about me.

If he doesn't hate me, he is well on his way to.

I hold Sarah to my chest as I stand. She is so light. Has she been losing weight? I'll need to make sure she is eating more. The jostle of my steps wakes Sarah, and her hand fists my shirt. "Where are we going?" Sarah's sleepy voice only softens my heart even more for her.

"I'm going to take you to your room, so you can sleep, doll."

She shakes her head, fluttering those long lashes up at me. The light catches the gold in her irises, and I almost trip and fall. Staring into her eyes is like staring at the rest of my future. It scares the living hell out of me. "No, I don't want to be alone, Jesse. Please," she begs, and those beautiful brown eyes start to drown in water.

I stop in the middle of the hallway. The only lights on are in the main room and the kitchen, and since we are in between, we are in the dark. If I continue straight, like I should if I'm smart, I'll place her in her room and shut the door behind me.

But apparently, I'm not a smart man because I take a left to my room instead. This is such a bad idea, and my mind is shouting at me to turn around and go back. Once she is in my room, in my bed, I know I'll want nothing else in life. I'll want to see her blonde hair splayed across the pillow and her lips parted as she waits for my kiss.

Yeah, this isn't a good idea, but no matter how much I chastise myself for taking another step, it feels right. I'm just a friend helping a friend, that's all. I open my door and cringe at the mess. I have clothes on the floor, drawers are halfway open with shirts hanging out, and my bed is a wreck.

"No, I don't want to lay where another woman laid last night."

I freeze halfway as I'm lowering her to the bed. "There was no woman here. Hasn't been a woman in a while, doll."

"Promise?" she asks, the innocence rolling off her tongue.

Who still asks for promises?

Someone who is too young for me, that's who.

"I swear it, doll. Get some sleep."

"Kiss me goodnight, Jesse."

I hate it when she says my name, but not because I don't like the sound of it. That's the problem. I love the sound of it. I've never heard my name fall off such sweet lips. "You know I can't do that, doll."

"I wish you would. Am I so bad?"

Where is all this coming from? She thinks I deny her because I don't find her attractive. This is the last thing we need to be worrying about. "Sarah, this is the last thing we need to be talking about, okay?"

It doesn't sit right with me to admit to any feelings I may have for her. She's fucking seventeen, for Christ's sake.

If that means denying and denying until she is eighteen, then so be it. It's a test of will I didn't know I had, but it's worth it. She doesn't understand now, but when she is eighteen, I'll make sure she understands why I had to do what I did.

"I'm going to go check on your brother." I lean down, hover my lips over hers, and move an inch to the left, pressing a kiss onto her heated cheek. "Go back to sleep." She's passed out by the time the words are out of my mouth. She hugs my pillow and tightens her arms around it, sighing as if she is the happiest woman on the planet.

I close the door softly as I leave and rub my eyes to wake up. I need some fucking coffee. I bypass the main room to get to the kitchen and wash my hands before I click the switch on each pot. Everyone is going to want a cup after the night we have had. I don't wait for the pot to fill. I grab a mug from the cabinet and fill it to the brim, and the liquid streaming out sizzles on the hot pad before I place the carafe back.

I take a sip, inhaling the steam coming from the black richness, and already the exhaustion slowly seeps out of my limbs and is replaced with new energy. I look toward the basement door, where Doc has set up his operating room, and debate if I want to go check what is going on. I don't want to interrupt him and make him mess up. That's the last thing I need on my shoulders.

When I get back into the living room, all the brothers are there, and a dead body is in the middle of the floor. *It's a good thing I took her to my room. Sarah doesn't need to see this.*

I do not feel like dealing with this. It's two in the fucking morning. I press against the bar, my hip taking most of my weight as I watch the guys bicker over what to do. I sip my coffee and wait for one of them to realize I'm here. I'm too tired to bark orders right now.

"No, he isn't cartel! He is the fucking mafia."

"And how do ye know that, Poodle? Just by looking at him?" Skirt sneers.

"We haven't had cartel problems here since the club formed. It isn't cartel."

For the first time, I agree with Poodle. "He's right. It isn't cartel," I say, pushing off the bar with my foot. "Cartel is careless. They would have driven by and did an up-close shot, not far away with a sniper rifle." I squat and turn the man's face in my direction. His shirt is off, and there are no tattoos that give away his affiliation. "I don't think he is mafia either. I think he was hired help."

"Why would the mafia want to do this? We have been in good business with them. Hell, I just got back from the casino, and the private rooms were booked. They have no reason to take us out," Tank states. "And who would want to hurt Boomer? He's just a kid."

"I don't think there was a target in mind. I think they were aiming at anyone they could as long as they took out one of our own." I stand and take another sip of coffee. It's sad that seeing a dead body feels like any other fucking day. "I need someone to call Badge. He might be able to run the cell phone records and fingerprints." Badge is the only one of us who's a cop. Some days, he turns the other way from what we do, and other days, he joins us. We toe the line of the law, but when we get too close, he backs off.

It can be murky waters sometimes, but I can't say it isn't convenient to have a Ruthless King on the inside with the police. Badge does a lot for us. "Burn the body. Keep the fingers so Badge can run them. Take his wallet and phone or anything else you find necessary to I.D. this guy." I'm considering bringing in a prospect who can do all that tech shit from here. I'm not trying to ruin Badge's career, and I know if he does too much for us, that's exactly what will happen. The MC isn't exactly on the department's nice list.

"How's Boomer, Prez?" Knives asks as he starts cutting away at the fingers. It helps that the guy is already dead. There won't be a mess since the blood stopped flowing.

I stare into the depths of my coffee and feel older than I have in a really long time. "I'm not sure. Doc is still working on him. Anyone with O negative or A negative blood, go donate. I'll be down in a minute."

Not many, but a good handful of men make their way

toward the basement door, and one by one they disappear as they descend the steps. I don't want to go down there and see the kid I practically raised hanging on to life. I'm not ready.

I knew when I took the position of being President things wouldn't be easy, but no one could have ever prepared me for it being this hard.

CHAPTER SEVEN

Sarah

I WAKE UP BY SOMEONE SHAKING MY SHOULDER. MY VISION IS BLURRY from sleep, so I scrub my fingers over my eyes to see Reaper in front of me. He looks so tired. I've never seen him look his age until right now. His shaggy hair is dirty, like he has run his fingers through it one too many times, he has dark circles under his eyes and new wrinkles on his forehead that weren't there the other day.

It's still dark out; only a trickle of the sun paints the sky giving it a muddled red hue. Red. Blood. Boomer. I sit up so fast, I don't register how close Reaper is to me and smack his forehead with mine. "Ow," I groan, holding my forehead as I fall back on the pillow. Of course, Reaper is unmoved like I didn't just whack him in the head with mine.

"You okay, doll?"

"You have such a hard head." My head swims a bit and the

thought of having a concussion crosses my mind for a split second, but my vision rights itself.

"I've been told," he says with a grim smile. "Boomer is out of surgery. He's stable. You want to see him?"

"He's alive?" I can't hold back the tears, and Reaper drops down beside me, grazing his knuckles over my cheeks.

"He's alive. He isn't awake, but he is alive," he tells me.

I throw myself at Reaper and hold him tight. I hardly remember anything from last night. I only remember being in complete panic and falling asleep in Reaper's arms. For a second, he doesn't hold me and again, rejection hits me. It's just a hug, and I'm not trying to throw myself at him right now. I'm relieved and want to hug someone with the happiness I feel.

"Can I go see him?"

He straightens to his full height, and I crane my neck back to look at him. He's such a big man. And after last night, I know that I have zero chance with him. I'll love him always, but maybe I need to tone it down.

Reaper holds out his massive hand. It has calluses all over it from time and hard work. His hands are stained with grease, and his nails are dirty. I guess for other women it would be unattractive, but not me; I find it attractive. I dream of those hands on my body and dirtying my flesh.

I slide my palm into his, and a spark of electricity has me gasping. I pull my hand back, but Reaper tightens his grip. And stupid me, I think it's because he wants to hold my hand, but then he helps me up and pushes me toward the door.

And then his hand is gone, leaving me a bit colder and little more alone than before. I open the door. The first thing I notice is how quiet the clubhouse is. Usually someone is up and walking around, drinking and causing havoc, but not this morning.

It's a ghost town. I gather my tangled blonde hair and throw it in a messy bun on top of my head as I make my way through the kitchen and to the basement door.

"I'll bring you coffee. You go ahead and go down there."

Like he has to tell me twice. I usually look back at Reaper as I walk away from him, but I'm feeling too rejected this morning, too tired, and too worried about my brother. My feet are bare against the old wooden slates of the steps. It smells like a hospital down here. Most basements are creepy, dark, and haunted with cobwebs and horror stories.

I'm sure this one does too, but at least this one has a good use. When I make it to the bottom step, I always get a little speechless when I see this room. It's set up like an emergency room. There are ten beds, all with their own machines and one is a surgical room. Reaper wanted to give Doc more, but with him being the only doctor in the club, it seemed pointless.

I see my brother in the middle of the room, the only one down here. The air is cold, and the faint beep of his heart rate monitor can be heard from the steps. Thank god it's even there.

"Sarah," Doc calls me over to where he stands in front of Boomer, clipping a chart to the bed. I don't see why Reaper couldn't talk to Doc about hiring a nurse or two. Doc is overworked. He pulls long hours here and at the hospital. There's only so much one man can do.

I get closer to Eric and see that even the name tag on his white coat says Doc. It makes me snicker internally. I don't understand why they can't just go by their names here. Some of them get so silly, like Poodle. Poor guy didn't ask for that. All because he has a poodle, the guys give him a hard time for it.

"Thanks for taking care of my brother." I engulf Eric in a big hug and squeeze. He doesn't hesitate to hug me back, like

Reaper does, and it feels nice. I don't feel that way toward Eric but feeling like I have a friend instead of being on the outside is a good change of pace. "How is he?" Gosh, I thought Reaper looked rough; it's nothing compared to what Eric looks like. The Doc has had better days. He looks dead on his feet.

I run over to the side of the bed and take Boomer's hand in mine. I want to give him a hug, but I'm too afraid I'll hurt him. I bend down and press our foreheads together. "Don't ever scare me like that again, okay?" I know Boomer can't answer me, but I can only hope he can hear me.

Eric's cheeks puff out as he exhales and then he yawns, stretching his arms over his head. "I'm sorry. It's been a long fucking night, but he is stable. I'm going to watch him for the next twenty-four hours. Right now, we want to watch for infection and clots, but I'm not worried. He should be alright. Don't just thank me, though. The guys really came through and donated a lot of blood. At least eight of them."

"Oh my god; I wanted to do that. I fell asleep." Guilt eats away at me. I shouldn't have cried myself to sleep. My brother needed me, and I acted like a child.

"If I really needed you, I would have woken you up. It was touch and go in surgery. Gunshot wounds to the abdomen can be hard to control, but I'm me, so I fixed it." He puffs out his chest, all proud just as he should be.

I lean up on my tiptoes and place my hand on his shoulders, giving him a kiss on the cheek. "You're a superhero in my book. Thank you so much."

"Ah." He rubs his cheek with his hand. "I'm just doing my job."

I run my hand down his arm until I can grip his hand and squeeze. "Why don't you go lay down and rest? I can stay down here with him. I want to visit with him anyway. If anything happens, I'll come wake you. You need to rest."

He seems unsure. Eric chews on his bottom lip and rocks back on the soles of his shoes. "I don't know. I really need to be quick to get to him. Seconds matter."

"Sleep in the bed next to him. I plan on reading him his favorite book. Maybe it will help you rest too."

"I'm not going to lie, that sounds fucking fantastic." He makes his way to the bed on the right of Boomer and sits down with a loud, overexuberant groan. "Oh my god, I haven't sat down in like fifteen hours."

"You need to take better care of yourself." I help him swing his feet on the bed and untie his shoes. "What if you mess up because you're too tired? You need to talk to Reaper about getting help down here. Maybe when I graduate, I'll try to get my nursing degree to help you. We can be a great team."

"You just worry about graduating first." He yawns.

The air conditioning kicks on, and I shiver, my teeth almost chattering. Has it not been on this entire time? Why is it so damn cold? I lift the blankets up to Eric's chin, and he scoffs but doesn't stop me from tucking him in like he is a little boy. I barely sit down before Eric is passed out and lightly snoring.

I sit between the two of them in a leather recliner and hold my brother's hand. Now that I feel like I'm by myself, I let go. I drop my forehead to the bed and pour out all the sorrow that has built in my chest. It's like I've unzipped my sternum, letting all the emotions spill out of me. My sobs, while I try to quiet them in the blanket on the bed, are still loud.

"I can't lose you too." I hold his hand against my cheek and remember the first time I saw him. He stared at me like I was up to no good, that I wasn't someone who needed help. He has always been so cynical, but then the moment he realized I was his sister, he changed. Sometimes, I think he is only here at this club for me. If I wasn't around, I don't think he'd be here. "You can't do that to me. You have no idea how much I need you. You can't leave me alone. You're the best part of my life now. Do you know how long I dreamed of having a life like this? I'd die, Boomer. I'd die if anything happened to you." Or, at least, losing him would feel like death.

A hand falls to my shoulder, and it doesn't startle me like usual. I know whose hand it is. I know the feel of it, the shape and width, the warmth, the strength of the fingers, I'd know them anywhere. "I brought you coffee," Reaper says, squeezing my shoulder before letting go.

He always let's go.

"Thank you," I tell him, never looking away from Boomer. Staring at my brother in the hospital bed, anger builds inside me when I think about Eric doing this all by himself. Eric saved my brother. Eric is working himself to death; does Reaper care? No. He only cares about himself. "You know…" I lean back and shake my head. "Eric deserves more than you give him. Boomer wouldn't be here if it wasn't for him. Look at him, Reaper, he can't keep doing this. Two hours of sleep here, two hours there; it isn't fair. You need to be better." I turn around and poke him in his chest. "So be better because Eric deserves better, and you know what? So does my brother. Eric is a good doctor, but any patient deserves a doctor well-rested. Either give the man a raise so he can quit his job or hire others. It really ticks me off that you have even waited this long. It's fucked up."

"Language," he says, but I know he isn't serious. I can hear the smile on his lips.

I take the coffee in my hand, and the heat makes the slight

chill in my body fade. I bring my nose to the ceramic cup and press the cold tip against it and sigh. It feels like winter down here.

Reaper lays a blanket on my lap and then tucks it under my chin. My arms are free so I can drink my coffee, but I'm already feeling better and it's because Reaper thought of me. Even if it was for a split second, he thought of me and got me a blanket.

I'm going to hold onto that.

"How is he doing?"

"Don't really know. Eric says he is stable and the next twenty-four hours are important, but he won't know more until after that."

"You're right." Reaper drags a chair across the room and settles next to me. "Eric does deserve better."

"What happened out there?" I ask, remembering the sound of the bullet. I jump, feeling like the moment is happening all over again.

Reaper doesn't answer right away. I wait patiently, drinking my coffee and watching my brother's chest rise and fall.

At least he is breathing.

"I don't have answers, but I promise you, I'm going to figure out who did this, and I'm going to put their heads on a stick."

I turn to him, keeping the blanket draped around me. I know Reaper will stay true to his word, but there is one thing I want him to save for me. "I want to be the one that puts his head on a stick. Can you do that?"

"Looks like you have a bit of Ruthless in your veins after all."

"I am my father's daughter," I say, reminding him that Boomer isn't the only one allowed to thirst for revenge.

CHAPTER EIGHT

Reaper

"WHO THE FUCK SENT THE HIT ON MY CLUB?" I RIP MY fist back and slam it against the face of the man who texted the sniper who shot my son. Cheekbones crush under my knuckles, and blood drips from the shattered face of this piece of shit human being. I've worked way too hard to build this MC up and keep it safe.

I've sent my men to the strip and hitting every casino we work with to get more information. I've had them double-check all the people we have forged documents like licenses, passports, and any other legal documents that could get flagged in the system for having a criminal background. I've even had them hit the other MC gang on the other end of the strip. No one knows anything. The mafia says they have nothing to do with it, but if there is one thing I have learned while being in this city it's that everyone lies.

I promised Sarah I wouldn't rest until I found the fucker

who nearly killed her brother, and I meant it. If it means I need to clean this city of lying fucks, then I will. Someone is lying to me, and I'm going to find out who, even if it means giving it my last fucking breath.

"Fuck. You." The man tied to the chair spits his blood and saliva in my face then grins. It's wicked looking since the blood is covering his teeth, and his lip is split, but if he is smiling, it means I haven't done enough.

"Fuck me?" I throw a punch to his gut, and he groans. I pull him back by the hair until the dirty black mane rips from his scalp. His nostrils flare as he swallows down the pain. I respect that. He's trying not to show weakness, but I know better than that. He is hurting right now, and it's only going to get worse until I get answers. "Fuck me?" I point a finger at my chest and toss my head back and laugh. It's loud and dramatic because what the fucker said isn't funny at all.

I walk over to the cart I have and look through my weapons of choice. I pluck the brass knuckles out and slide them onto my fingers. "I'm going to give you one last chance." I bend down until I know he can smell the beer pouring off my lips. I've been drinking it between punches. Torturing someone works up a thirst. I grip his chin, squeezing the bone so hard that he whimpers like the little bitch I know he is. "Your number was the last number on the phone of the guy my men killed. The guy who almost killed my son. I have a feeling you know him." I let go of his face that's sweat and blood soaked. Tongue and Bullseye are in the corner off to the side of the surgical room.

I had to have my own space when we redid the basement for Doc. It's soundproof, and every inch of the walls and floor are stainless steel. There's a drain in the middle and a hose hooked on top of the ceiling for easy cleanup.

Things get messy when you're trying to make a point.

"If I say anything, he'll kill me."

"And if you don't say anything, I'll kill you." I graze the knuckles over his split cheek. I can see the bone peeking out, and it makes me feel a bit giddy on the inside.

"You're fucking crazy."

I punch him across the face, and he sobs when his nose breaks. He gasps for air, and blood fills his throat from how much I just fucked up his nose. It's crooked, and not even resetting it will make it better. "You haven't seen crazy. Do you taste the blood dripping down your throat? You feel it bubbling? It's only the beginning if you don't tell me what I want to hear..." I reach for his wallet that is next to his phone on the counter and open it. "Alex Torres from... Oh, guys, look, we have a local. Born and raised right here in Vegas."

"Maybe you can show us around sometime," Bullseye says. "I've been meaning to sightsee more."

"Me too," Tongue says simply.

I grip the man's face again, and dark red blood spills from his lips. I force his head to the side, and his eyes land on Tongue, who is currently licking the sharp blade he has in his hand. "You see that man right there, Mr. Torres? Do you know what he does for me?"

His head doesn't move, but his eyes slide to mine, a sliver of fear shining back at me. Good. He needs to be scared.

"He cuts the tongues out of all our enemies. I bet you'd love to speak again, wouldn't you? Whisper those sweet little nothings as you have sex with a woman and try to have her orgasm with your pathetic cock?" I grin. "He isn't afraid to cut that off too. My man here is a guy of many talents." It isn't often that I threaten a man's junk because the thought has me cringing, but the first thing I did when Bullseye tied this fucker up was to undress him. I want this asshole to feel vulnerable in every way, and when I get the answers I want...

I may consider letting him live.

Maybe.

Depends on how I feel.

"And you want to know what I love to do?" I take a step back, letting go of his face. I grab a very sharp scalpel from my arsenal of goodies and spin it around in my fingers. "Not many people know this about me, okay?" The light glints off the silver metal as I bring it down to his chest and carve out a shallow shaped heart, right where his heart lies. He screams with every second my blade is against his skin.

The red beads and drips down his chest, pooling in his navel. Sweat drips from his hair, onto his bare thighs as his head drops. "I like to cut out the beating hearts of the ones who fuck me over, Alex. It's why they call me Reaper. I like to watch you, watch me, watch your heart beat in my hand and feel your soul sink into my palm on the very last effort your heart gives to stay alive."

"You're a sick motherfucker!" the man yells and pulls at the restraints on his wrists. It's no use. He has straps over his shins, thighs, and chest, and that doesn't include the iron cuffs we have on his wrists. "Let me out of here!"

And now the screams begin.

It isn't often I get to do what I'm named after because everyone thinks what Tongue does is the worst. Only a handful of men know what my poison is in the club, and that's how it is going to stay.

"Are you going to tell me what I want to know?" I ask, taking a step back and laying the scalpel down on the cart.

Before I ever take out the hearts, I let my guys have their way too. Some pains get more information than others. I only take the heart when I know I won't get any information, but this man will break. I see it in his eyes.

"You'll have to kill me," he spits again, and it lands on my boots.

Damn it. I just polished them.

"Oh, we will have our fun first, though, okay?" I wave at Bullseye, who is known for his impeccable aim. He pulls the sharp metal darts from his pocket. He has a line painted on the floor, ten feet back. Regulations are seven feet and nine inches, but he is so damn good, he steps back another two feet.

The man glances around frantically, staring at all of us one by one. "Wha—what is he doing? What's that in his hand?"

I pat the man's head and stand directly beside him as Bullseye gets into position. "That is Bullseye. He loves to play darts. The heart I carved into you?" I jerk his head back and snarl, "He is going to aim for it." I push him forward again, and Tongue chuckles. It's slow and raspy, just like his voice, and damn if it doesn't sound maniacal.

"What the fuck is wrong with you people?"

I sigh, stepping in front of him and place my boots between his legs on the chair. "I'll tell you what's wrong with me…" I shove the chair, and it falls back, slamming against the floor, and the metal vibrates from the force. I walk around him and squat, pressing my boots directly on his face. All it would take is a swift kick or my entire body weight to crush his head in. That's it.

Poof.

He'd be gone.

"My problem is that you think it's okay to keep information. You realize you know who almost killed a nineteen-year-old kid, right? You're okay with that?"

He sniffles. He fucking sniffles and cries. "Man, I wasn't directly a part of it. I swear to god. I swear."

"Now we are getting somewhere, Alex." I shove my boot under the back of the chair and push it upward until it lands on its legs. Getting this guy to talk is harder than I expected. When Badge said he had the guy in the back of his car who spoke to the man who shot Boomer, I was stunned, relieved, and ready to get this shit over. I have my hands in many things, and the last thing I need is someone trying to start a war with me.

They would lose.

I'm a fucking gladiator, and anyone who comes up against me, I'll kill without blinking.

"Talk to me. What do you know?" I cross my arms, and Bullseye throws a dart that whizzes by Alex's head. The man's eyes are wide as they shift to the right. He must have felt the wind from the dart passing his head. "He doesn't miss. He's just upset that he doesn't get to play."

"Fuck yeah I am. I haven't had a human dartboard in like, three months. I'm rusty."

"I haven't cut out any tongues in a while. It's sad." Tongue sighs longingly at his blade, as if she is a mistress he hasn't seen and wants to make love to again.

"Okay, okay, I'll tell you what I know, but you guys have to protect me. They will kill me if I say anything."

"They aren't here right now threatening your life; we are. I think you better worry about us first. And I'm not protecting you. My son is out there healing from a fucking gunshot wound from your friend. You're on your own after this."

"Please," he begs. "Please, I'll do anything." The smell of piss fills the air, and Alex's body starts to shake. His urine flows to the middle of the room since the floors are slanted an inch, inverting in the middle.

"Fuck, that stinks," Bullseye waves a hand in front of his face. "You need to drink more water."

We haven't been the best hosts. I haven't given him food or water, and it's been two days. I like to deprave captives when they're in my hands. The more desperate they are, the more honest they are.

And I'm just looking for the truth.

"You can get water once you tell me what you know. That's a deal." I open the fridge in the corner, take a new plastic bottle full of filtered cold water, and set it on the counter where all my weapons of choice are. "Speak, don't beg. I'm getting impatient."

"Okay, okay." Alex spits more blood out from his mouth and takes a deep breath in since he can't breathe through his nose. "The man who came here the other night, his name was Sebastian. I hadn't heard from him, so I assumed he got found."

"Damn right he did." Bullseye throws another dart, harder this time, and the zing it makes as it zips by Alex's head makes him whimper and cower into himself.

"Your friend is dead," I say, keeping my voice even and uncaring.

"I figured as much." He swallows and inhales again. "Fabian Trullo hired him."

"Fabian Trullo," Bullseye repeats. "Why do I know that name?"

"He is the stepson of Mateo Moretti," Alex mumbles.

"Holy shit, you've got to be kidding me." Bullseye folds his hands behind his head. "I thought we were good with them, Prez?"

"You're sure about that? Moretti is behind this?" I ask the bleeding, begging prisoner. That's the mafia boss here in Vegas. As far as I know, we are on good terms. We work together, we keep the city clean, do a few favors for each other. We get more done together than we would constantly battling against one another. So we struck a truce. He offers his help when I need it and vice versa.

"I don't know if it was Moretti. His stepson is an asshole. Word is he is trying to form his own business to branch away from the Moretti name."

"No way would the mafia turn their backs on us." Bullseye stands in front of me, keeping his voice low so Alex can't hear him.

I don't believe that for a second. Mafia are a dangerous crowd, and when they want change, they implement it. I'm not sure if this is a warning or a threat from Moretti, or a move from his stepson to try to show power. Either way, I need to retaliate. "I wouldn't be too sure about that, Bullseye. Trust is something born within families, not truces." I trust my MC, but people outside of it… Never.

"You think Moretti would be dumb enough to do that to you?"

"After what he did to the first club owner to get near us? I don't think there is anything he wouldn't do. And let's not forget what he did to the President of the Vegas Vipers." When I found the head of the man on my doorstep with a note that said 'Truce,' Moretti and I haven't had one damn problem since.

"So I can live now, right? I told you everything you needed to know." Alex nods and gives us a swollen grin filled with hope.

"I did say that, didn't I?" I say with a click of my tongue. "Bullseye? Do the honors."

Bullseye gives me a knowing look before going back to the line he painted across the room.

"I swear, I won't tell a soul what happened here."

"I know you won't," I say and nod toward Bullseye.

He flicks the small metal dart through the air, making it look as easy as a snap of the finger, and the sharp needle lands directly in the heart I carved in Alex's chest, no doubt piercing the organ beating underneath it.

"You—you—said—" Alex can't finish his sentence, and he struggles to stay alive while his heart furiously pumps around the needle penetrating it.

I grip the back of his neck and tilt my lips to the side, acting disappointed in myself. "Yeah, I lied." I don't carve out his heart while it's still beating. He did tell me what I needed to know, so I won't give him too much of a painful death. It's nice of me. His pupils go from sharp points to large black circles once the life leaves him. I stand, popping my neck and back from the last few hours of stress.

"Thought you didn't like liars?" Bullseye plucks the dart from Alex's chest and wipes his blood on his jeans.

"Never trust someone who *can* lie."

His brows wrinkle as he ponders what I said, and Tongue steps from the shadows, a place he seems to live these days, and says what Bullseye must be thinking, "But everyone can lie."

"Exactly."

Never trust a soul. Never trust a tongue. People will make anything they say sound pretty and, more often than not, they pay for the ugly truth that lies underneath.

CHAPTER NINE

Sarah

"**S**ARAH."
My name is whispered in the back of my dreams.

"Sarah," the voice croaks. It's deep and sleepy, almost sounding like a struggle. "Wake up, sis."

The voice sounds familiar, feels familiar. It draws me out of my dream, and the closer I get to consciousness, the further away the voice gets. My head drops from the mattress, and I jerk awake, catching myself right before I fall out of the chair and on the floor.

"Well, hey, sleeping beauty."

The sound of my brother's voice replaces all the caffeine in the world. "Boomer! You're awake!" I throw my arms around him as much as I can without hurting him. He grunts from the bounce of the bed, but he manages to wrap his hands around my back. Tears roll down my face with pure joy. When Eric told me all the complications of post-surgery, I could hardly sleep. I worried myself to death until finally exhaustion took hold and sucked me under. "I was so scared I was going to lose you."

He drops his arms and pulls away from me to lay back down. He looks so tried, and he has only been awake for a few minutes. "It's going to take more than a bullet to get me down."

"I don't know. That bullet took you down pretty hard. I thought you were dead."

"I didn't say it didn't hurt." He winces when he tries to sit up on his own, and little beads of sweat break out over his forehead. He is pale, eyes dark and sunken in, and his lips are a bit chapped. His dark brown eyes usually carry a golden hue, but not today; not while he is in pain and weak. His hair needs a good washing and, to be honest, he kind of stinks.

I fan my hand in front of my face and grimace. "You smell."

His stomach shakes, and something between a laugh and a groan escapes him. "Way to kick a man while he is down. I can't help that I smell, and it isn't like I can bathe myself."

"I can give you a sponge bath." He goes to interrupt me, but I shove my hand over his mouth. "Just listen to me. You can keep your boxers on and the blanket over your ... you know. I don't want to see that anyway. Gross. I'm just saying, I can help. Let me, please." At this point, I want to do anything to help. I have never been in the position to actually care for someone before.

It's always just been about me, trying to survive, trying to make it to the next day. I didn't have the energy to worry about anyone other than me. Bouncing around from foster home to foster home, the parents were either in it for the check or most of the time they were absent. Some of the kids were bullies themselves, and I couldn't blame them; not when life had been so cruel.

And then I landed at my last foster home, where the man videotaped my beatings. Not just mine, but other kids before me. He recorded the kill too. The sick fuck liked to re-watch what he did to us over and over again. The least I can do for Boomer is help him bathe, especially when he killed the man who nearly took my life.

I can see the reluctance in the shadows of his eyes, but eventually he gives a small tilt of his head.

"I'll be right back with your stuff, sponge, and a bowl, okay? Don't go anywhere." I snort. "Duh, you can't."

"You little bitch." He smiles and tries to throw a pillow at me, but it falls short since he has no strength, and it hits the foot of the bed. "Go. And can you bring back some water? I'm dying down here. And something to eat?"

"I'll bring water and soup, nothing too heavy."

"Thanks, Sarah. I don't know what I'd do without you." His eyes open and close slowly as he fights sleep. "You're the only reason—" but he doesn't finish his sentence. Exhaustion wins, and he falls peacefully asleep. I won't wake him. I'll still go upstairs and get the necessary items together, grab a book, and head back down to be with him. I haven't left his side over the last two days, except when Reaper came down and told me to get upstairs because he had some club business to attend to down here.

And with the man they had dragging behind him, I assumed club business was nothing good.

My hand slides up the stainless-steel rail as I climb the steps. When I open the basement door and make my way into the kitchen, I notice all the windows open. A fresh breeze comes through, swaying the red curtains. The smell of the earth, hot and dry, makes me wish for it to rain. It's the desert for a reason, though, rain isn't something that comes here often.

I rummage through the cabinets, looking for the soups and canned good. Even after a year, I haven't been able to learn where things are yet, and it isn't because I don't pay attention. It's because these men don't put shit back in the same spot twice. No matter how many times I rearrange it or label it, they just throw shit wherever they want.

For instance, why is the silverware in the drawer where the potholders are? I made a separate place for it. It drives me bonkers.

"What are you doing?"

Reaper's voice always startles me when he comes out of nowhere. I bang my head on the cabinet and groan, rubbing the spot where the edge of the wood hit me.

"Shit, are you okay?" His concern makes my heart trip and melt. Reaper pulls my hand away and drags my head out of the cabinet where I was looking for soup. "Let me see it."

"I'm fine." I bat his hand away, hating that even the briefest of touches from him makes my body run wild.

A stern expression falls over his face. His thick eyebrows furrow a bit, and his lips press into a line. "I'll be the one to determine that. Let me see. I won't say it again."

I'm not sure why, but it sounds like a threat should come after that. So I run with it. "And if you have to? What will you do? Spank me?"

His eyes turn to fire and before I can annoy him more, he spins me around and parts my hair. "I'll spank you again. I'm sure you remember the first time."

I do remember the first time, and it was awful. It wasn't

pleasurable—it was meant for punishment. A cold dose of reality drenches me and makes my bones shiver from the memory of the rejection. I was only sixteen, so I understood why he did it.

"You're fine. You might have a bump, but you'll live."

I reach into the cabinet and wrap my fingers around the cool can and bring it out. I close the cabinets only to open another one next to it to grab a bowl. "Jeez, don't sound too disappointed." I slam the cabinet harder than I should and get the can opener from another cabinet, slamming that too. I swear, sometimes I wonder if Boomer and I should leave, and then I wouldn't have to love Reaper and see him every damn day. Maybe then he wouldn't be so annoyed with me, and his life will be better. That's how he acts. It's like I'm this huge burden, and it's starting to wear me down.

"Hey, what the fuck? I wouldn't ever want that. You make me feel like such a bad guy, Sarah."

The electronic can opener buzzes as I grab the countertop and hang my head. "You aren't a bad guy. You're the best guy I know. I don't really feel like getting a lecture from you, okay?" It's the same talk, different day. Any time I hit on him or rub against him, he gives me the "you're too young for me" talk and honestly, I'm in the mood to dish it, not take it.

Another gust comes through the window and dries out my eyes, so I glance away and pour the soup in the bowl, throw it in the microwave, and press start. Instead of a glass of water, I pull out a pitcher and fill it full of ice and filtered water. I don't want Boomer to have to worry about not having anything to drink.

"You need to grow up, Sarah. Life is full of lectures, and you only get so many because you don't seem to be taking in anything I'm saying."

"Oh, I'm taking it in, Reaper. It's loud and clear as fucking day. I'm getting food for Boomer; I don't want to talk about this right now." I hit my fist against the counter, doing all I can to make sure I don't punch him across the face. The man is maddening.

"Well, that's too fucking bad." He spins me around by my arm and grips my wrist tight, pinning it to the counter. "Stop throwing yourself at me. I'm too—"

"Old? I'm too young? I know. I've heard it before. I've heard it a hundred times, Jesse."

"Then why won't you listen to me?" He takes my other hand in his, trapping me with his body against the sink. A bit of water from where I filled up the pitcher soaks through the back of my shirt since I didn't wipe it off the counter. "I'm begging you to listen to me. Why must you fight me every chance you get?" His words are soft and a bit broken, as if it hurts for him to speak them. Reaper's hold loosens around my wrists, but he doesn't let go. "Stop fighting me," he pleas, laying his forehead on mine. It's a tender gesture, one that gives me hope, one that, for the first time, makes me wonder if he does have feelings for me.

"No," I reply to him, my lips so close to his I can almost taste the coffee lingering on his breath.

His face pinches as if my defiance causes him pain. "Answer me this. Why?"

Why? Because I love you.

But I can't say that, not yet; it will only create a massive trench in the slight crack of our relationship.

"I'll fight you until you realize we don't need to fight any-more," I answer, leaning into his hard body more than I should.

More than he ever allows.

I'm tired of fighting him. If he thinks I actually get pleasure out of trying to throw myself at him and getting rejected at every turn, he has another think coming. More often than not, I cry myself to sleep from the humiliation I feel, from the longing I feel for him because for so long I've had these feelings, and it wasn't reciprocated on his end.

"You're a maniac, Sarah. There are too many reasons why this can't happen." Reaper presses his forehead against mine before pushing away from me. He releases my wrists, and I immediately miss the pressure.

I'm wearing him down. I see it in his face. He is so damn handsome. His temples are starting to gray, but other than that, he has a head full of thick hair that matches his scruff on his face. Today, he is wearing a simple white shirt with his cut, and on the left breast is a patch that says 'President.' There are a few grease stains splattered along his jeans that are torn along the knees, and his boots are scuffed to hell, but I know they're his favorites because he chooses them out of all the others he has.

"I don't care about any of the reasons. Not a single one."

He throws his hands on his hips and stares at the ceiling, chuckling. "Well, I care."

"I don't care that you care."

"That's what worries me. Keep this in mind—you're underage, and I won't have you ruining my life; are we clear?"

"If I were to ruin your life, I'd be ruining mine too. So why would I?" I take a step forward, not to where we are touching again because I know he wouldn't like that. I can tell he is on the edge, and I don't want him to stomp away, mad at me. I just want to be able to feel his warmth again. And is he that afraid he will give into me?

If he ever did, I wouldn't tell a soul. I wouldn't deny him, and I think that's what most of his problem is and why he fights this thing between us.

Tool takes that moment to walk in, and I take a step back, but it isn't missed by Tool that something was going on before he ruined it.

Fucking, Tool.

"Prez? I have more information, and Moretti got your message. He wants to talk."

"Good," Reaper grunts and almost trips over the dining room chair as he walks away from me. Tool gives him a funny look, lifting his brow, but he doesn't say anything else as he vanishes down the hallway.

Reaper takes an apple from the brown bowl in the center of the table, tossing it in the air before catching it again. He's leaving without saying anything. What else is there to say?

"Reaper?" I never call him that, at least not to his face.

He pauses the bite in the apple, and when he turns to me, the big red piece of fruit silences his 'huh', making it all muted and mumbled.

I turn around, grab the bowl of soup and the pitcher of water, and leave the man I'm in love with first, so he can watch me walk away. "I'm your maniac."

The crunch of the apple makes me grin, and then it's followed by a thump on the floor and a curse. Huh, looks like someone needs another apple.

CHAPTER TEN

Reaper

"**W**HAT'S GOING ON WITH THAT?" TOOL ASKS ME AS WE walk out of the saloon doors of the clubhouse.

I hate to say it, but I think the saloon doors are going to have to go. With this new threat, I want to make sure the club is a fortress. Over the last few years, threats haven't been a concern; things have been running so fucking smoothly that it's been a dream.

But too much of a good thing...

"What was what?"

"Reaper, what the fuck are you doing?"

I lean against the rail of the porch, the wood hot from the afternoon sun. The heat doesn't stop me from craving a cigarette. Opening my cut, I dip my hand in the inner pocket and take the pack of smokes out. After I pack the case by hitting it against my palm, I place the sweet nicotine between my lips and light it with a match. "I don't know what you're talking about." I know damn well what he is talking about, but what happened in the kitchen, shouldn't have happened.

"Do I need to be worrying about you? Are you fucking her?"

I blow smoke in his face at the same time I press my elbow against his throat, and I lean into him until his back must be killing him from the pressure the rail is putting on him. "I'm going to say this once—whatever is, or isn't, happening, isn't your fucking business. I'm not fucking her, or will I ever fuck her. I'm not stupid."

A sharp inhale from behind me churns my stomach. When I look at Tool, his eyes are locked on the saloon doors, and when he glances over at me, I know it isn't one of the cut-sluts standings there, but Sarah.

Out of all the times she has to follow me, why does it have to be now? My arm falls from Tool's neck, and he rubs the irritated flesh while mean mugging me. He fucking deserved it. I try to steer the conversation away from what she overheard like an idiot. "How's your brother?" I ask. I take a hit on the cigarette between my lips, but the damn nicotine doesn't do its job and calm my nerves. I'm a raging mess inside because I see the tears threatening to fall.

"Asleep," she informs me and takes a step outside with me and Tool.

Having her in the same vicinity is starting to become too difficult. The next few months can't go by fast enough. When she turns eighteen, I won't feel so fucking guilty for wanting someone younger than me. And damn it, I fucking want her so goddamn bad. What makes it harder is that she doesn't even look seventeen. She has long, luxurious hair that curls at the end over her small breasts, and her waist is lean with a steep curve in the middle before it rounds to her hips and ass. Her lips are pouty all the fucking time, swollen and plump, and her eyes are wide naturally, and almost too big for her face.

She's gorgeous and will only get prettier as she gets older.

"Good, good. I'm glad he is resting." Awkward silence falls, and I inhale a long drag of the cigarette.

"Am I really so bad?" she asks, breaking my damn heart with every word.

Before I can defend myself, she takes off down the steps, sprinting across the parking lot. When she gets next to my bike, she runs past it then stops.

"Don't even think about it!" I shout, stopping on the third step of the porch as I watch her take a step backward, look at my beautiful bike, and lift her leg.

She kicks it. In slow motion, I watch my bike fall to the ground, and Tool gasps from the horrific sight. I hear the scrapping of rocks against the custom paint. It's a biker's worst fear to see their motorcycle on the ground.

Then the little psychopath stomps on the fuel tank.

"Oh god. Ow, that hurts me." Tool cringes, holding his stomach as if it is personally happening to him.

That's what it feels like. A personal beating.

I stomp down the steps, and before I can pick up the pace, she is darting away and across the street, climbing over the large hill. "Where the fuck are you going?" I shout after her and change my jog to a sprint.

"Fuck. You!" she screams and disappears over the hill.

Damn it. I can't let her get too far. It's the damn desert, and it's hot as hell out here. She can get lost, and I'll never see her again. The thought has me running full speed, and I jump onto the mound of dirt. My boots slide against the red clay until they gain traction, and my fingers dig into the hot dirt, getting trapped under my fingernails as I pull myself up the damn hill.

"What the hell?' Tool asks from below.

I'm on top of the hill now, surrounded by cactuses and dead bushes fried from the sun. There's a small moving dot a few yards ahead of me, and instead of coming closer, she's going further. "That little...." I run down the hill and shout, "Tell the boys if we aren't back by dark to come looking for us." I don't bother looking back. I keep my eyes forward on the dot in front of me. It's hard to run in steel-toe boots, but I'm so used to it by now, it's second nature.

It's nearing a hundred degrees right now. I've only been running for a minute, and already sweat has drenched my entire body. It's too hot for this shit. When I get ahold of her, I'm going to skin her fucking hide. Sarah gives me such a damn headache.

But life wouldn't be the same without her.

If she wants to run, I'll chase her.

And when I catch her, there will be hell to pay.

"Sarah! Stop this shit!" I yell and jump over a prickly looking bush that I know would hurt if I landed on it. I'd be picking pins out of my ass for a month.

"Fuck off, Jesse!" she responds, her legs moving quicker than mine as they kick up dust.

They might move quicker, but I have longer strides.

"Will you stop?" I shout again. It's too damn complicated to yell and run in this heat. My sweat is stinging my eyes, and the sun is blinding me. I can't let her get away because she's so damn stubborn. I know she won't come back, and then she will be lost. I won't let her die in this heat and be bones forgotten in the sand like so many others.

I'm just about to reach for her and swing her into my arms when she trips and falls onto the ground, crying out when she catches most of her weight on her arms. I try to come to a complete stop, but I'm going too fast, and my boots don't catch the ground. I slide and fumble, slowing when I almost fall. My fingertips skim the ground, and when I right myself, I turn around and head straight through a cloud of dust.

I cover my mouth and cough when I inhale all the dust swirling. Since there is no wind, the cloud settles quickly. That's when I see Sarah, sitting with her arms wrapped around her legs. She's crying. I fall to my knees, uncaring of the rocks and shit digging into me. Her arms are bleeding from the scrapes she sustained from the fall.

"Sarah—"

She scrambles back on her hands and feet, her ass sliding against the ground as she shakes her head. "Don't touch me!"

I have never seen her like this before. The look on her face is one of betrayal and heartbreak. Fat tears roll down her face, ruining her mascara and causing long black lines down her cheeks. Her lips are red and swollen, and her bottom lip is bleeding too; probably because she's been chewing on it. She does that when she cries.

"Sarah, we need to go home."

"I don't want to go anywhere with you."

Her youth is starting to shine through. A grown woman who has been in love and has experienced heartache would never act like this. They know how much love can hurt, but they don't run into the desert to forget it; at least, I don't think they do.

As a matter of fact, I don't know much about women

except how to fuck 'em, so maybe I need to keep my thoughts to my damn self.

"Stop acting like—"

"A child?" she finishes my sentence for me. "That's what I am, right? A child. Don't put your hands on me, Reaper. I am not going back with you. I want nothing to do with you or the club, and when my brother can finally walk, we are leaving."

I know that Jenkins has been on the fence with me for a few years now, especially with Sarah living with us. He has always had this way about him, like he tolerates the club but hates it at the same time. It's why I haven't given him his father's cut for him to prospect. If he doesn't seem like he wants it, then why would I give it to him?

"Why would you do that? Why would you leave me?" I mean to ask why they would want to leave me when I've done nothing but provide for them, take care of them, protect them, and love them.

I love her, and I'm just waiting until she is legal. Why is that so hard for her to understand?

"You don't mean that!" I fall to my knees in front of her and take her hands in mine. "Sarah, you don't mean that. You're angry right now, and I understand—"

"No, no! You don't understand. I don't get you at all. We share moments. I know it isn't all in my head. I feel it," she cries, placing her hand above her heart. "I feel you all the time, right here. You've made yourself home inside me, Jesse."

There it is. I love it when she calls me Jesse. Reaper doesn't sound right when she says it. I think it's because no one else ever calls me that, and I hate it, but every time she says it, I just want to kiss her.

"So when I hear you say you'd never have sex with me

because you just aren't that stupid, it hurts. It hurts more than you will ever know. Am I so disgusting that you can't even imagine having sex with me?"

If I'm honest, I'm a bad man.

If I lie, I'm a bad man.

This is why trust is so hard to come by.

Sarah's laugh is full of irony when I stay silent. "My god, are you really not even going to answer me? No one else is around, Jesse! We are literally alone in the fucking desert. No one can hear you. God, you are unbelievable. You can be the man everyone else wants you to be, but I expect one thing from you—one—and you can't even give me that. You can give everyone else everything, but me? I'm begging for scraps. You make me feel like a fucking dog—a bitch, to be exact." She gets up and heads west, which is once again nowhere near the clubhouse, but in the direction of the strip.

Her words piss me off. I march to her and snake my arm around her, holding her to my body. She doesn't fight me. She has no energy to. Her thin shirt is wet with sweat, and her chest rises and falls from the exertion of this entire ordeal. I glance down to see the sweat glimmering off her golden skin, and a droplet runs down between her palm-sized tits.

I want nothing more than to lick it off her skin and taste to see if she is salty or sweet. Fuck! I can't. I can't for another few months.

She wiggles against me to try to get out of the hold I have her in, but I'm much stronger than she is. The more she fights me, the harder it is to control my cock. It's been a full year since I've had another woman under me, against me, kissing me, sucking me, because every time I close my eyes, brown ones stare back at me.

"You feel that?" I press my pelvis against her. I can't believe in this heat I can manage to get my cock up, but with Sarah, I can be on my death bed and still get an erection. "Is that what you want to know? Is that what you want to feel?" I push her away from me and roar into the air. I'm so frustrated. She has me all bent and twisted. I'm the President of the Ruthless Kings; I'm not supposed to be all fucked up inside. "Fuck, Sarah! You think it's easy for me? You think it's easy for me to see you every fucking day and not do a damn thing about it?" I pace and start worrying a trench in the dirt. With a shake of my head, I stop right in front of her. "You think I want this? I don't want to want you, Sarah; get that through your head. When I say you're too fucking young, I mean it. You are too young. You keep throwing yourself at me, begging me to take you, and I won't. I refuse to, but don't think for one fucking minute that not being able to have you, the way you want me to, doesn't kill me every second because it does. I'm an old man compared to the boys your age. I've lived my life. I have nothing to offer you, but guess what? I'm counting down the fucking days, crossing them off my goddamn calendar until your birthday. So get this shit out of your head right now because in two months, you'll be mine—that I can fucking promise you. Until then, stop fighting me." My chest is heaving when I'm done yelling, and that's when I notice how close I am. I've bent my head down until my lips are close to hers; a soft wind could blow me over and make us finally touch.

I do one of the hardest things I've ever had to do.

I take a step back from my little maniac.

CHAPTER ELEVEN

Sarah

H E TAKES A STEP AWAY FROM ME, CARRYING A PIECE OF MY HEART with him. It's unbearable. Now that I know he actually cares about me, I can breathe easier. I feel crazy for acting the way I did, but it was like my lungs got ripped from my body, and I wasn't able to breathe after I overheard what he said to Tool, his VP.

I stare off into the distance; the sun setting over the tall buildings on the strip is something I'll never forget. I need to come out here more. The reds and oranges painting the sky seem darker than when I'm watching them from the clubhouse. It is more isolated out here, lonelier, and maybe that's why the colors look so different. I've never seen them before, not like this.

"I'll never stop fighting for you, Jesse," I say as a hint of the breeze blows. I cross my arms under my breasts when the chill of the night starts to inch its way in the air.

His palm lands on my lower back before jerking away and leaving me alone again. "No need to fight for me, doll. Okay? You have what you wanted to know. The fight can be over."

He doesn't know, but it's only just begun between us now that I know he actually wants me.

"We need to get home. I told the guys if we weren't back by dark, to come looking for us. I'd rather get you home than have a flock of them come searching."

He holds out his hand, and I stare at it, not knowing what he wants me to do. His fingers are so long and thick, and bold black lines swirl over the tops of his hands and up his arms. He wiggles his fingers, and I do the only thing that I think of.

I give him a high five.

"What are you doing?"

"You're the one holding your hand out. What else am I supposed to do with it?" I ask, staring at the outstretched hand as if it's an alien.

"Well, you could hold it."

I don't think I heard him right. Why would he want to hold my hand? Isn't that crossing one too many lines that he has drawn in the sand? This has to be some kind of joke; payback for the tantrum I just pulled.

"This is a one-time deal for the next two months. No one is around. No one can see. I'll hold your hand until we get closer to the road. I want to, but then things go back to the way they were. We have your prom, your graduation, and then your birthday."

"Sounds like you've been making a list."

"And checking it fucking twice," he mutters under his breath. "Are you going to take my hand or not?"

Do I look like an idiot? I'd never miss a chance to hold

his hand. I unwrap my arms from my chest, and with a shaky hand, I reach for his. I stop midway, waiting to see if he is playing a joke, but when he doesn't move, I slide my hand into his and lock our fingers together. Our palms touch, and a wave of calm washes over me.

Finally.

Finally!

"Looks like someone stopped fighting me." I look up at him through my eyelashes, and I have to squint.

"The fight hasn't even started yet. Come on; let's go home. I'm sure everyone is worried sick about you."

"Right," I snort as we start walking toward the direction of the clubhouse. "Everyone would be happier if I wasn't there." I let what I have been really feeling off my chest in a blasé tone.

He tugs my hand as he comes to a stop. "You can't mean that? You really think the guys would be better off? That I'd be better off?"

I lift a shoulder and shrug, blowing a piece of hair out of my face. "You can't say it isn't true. You and the guys haven't really had a break. You raised Boomer, and then I fell on your doorstep. How long has it been since you've actually been able to act like the club you used to be?"

"If I wanted the club the way it used to be, I'd have it be that way. Do you want the cut-sluts coming around and fucking every man in sight? We can party every night, go out on more runs, and I plan to have all that back, when you turn eighteen. The guys know the deal. If they don't like it, they can leave. I won't subject a kid to shit like that, not if I can help it." He lets go of my hand and cups my face instead. "Don't you dare for one second think we'd be better off without you. You bring something special that none of us have ever had, that I have never had."

"And what's that?" I lay a hand on top of his and lean into it, hoping the moment never ends. Why can't we just stay out here all night and watch the stars? We can hold each other, and it can remain our secret.

He brushes his nose against mine and drops his hands from my face. "You aren't old enough to know that yet. Come on."

I take his hand again, and as we walk, I notice his strides are slower. I have a stupid grin on my face the entire way home. My cheeks hurt. For the first time in my life, I have this giddy feeling in my stomach, and I just might explode from it. It's more than all the times I've tried to jump Jesse's bones. I know now it isn't one-sided and it's like I'm walking on the moon.

We steal a few glances at each other as we take our time. He shakes his head when he meets my gaze again and then rubs his fingers through his hair like he can't believe what he is doing.

"You have to stop looking at me like that," he says.

"Like what?"

"You're too young to know that too."

"Jesse, I'm almost eighteen. I know about sex. I know about a lot of things."

He growls, a threatening rumble in his chest that makes a flicker of fear present inside me. "I don't want to hear about how you know those things. We can't be talking about this. Don't. I'm already doing one thing I shouldn't be doing." He squeezes my hand, the interaction innocent but forbidden.

I'm not going to argue or ruin the only chance I have at being close to him, so I do what he says and keep my trap freaking shut. I'm in my own happy world, daydreaming of the life Jesse and I are going to have, imagining all the kids running around who look just like him, when we come to the hill that takes us back to reality.

It's silly. On one side, he has to act like he doesn't want me; on this side of the hill, we can do whatever we want. What's the rush? Why do we need to go back?

"Club ain't going to run itself. We gotta go." He tries to let go of my hand, but I hold on tight, afraid that once we cross this boundary, he'll forget all about me. What if he said those things just to make me feel better?

"Come on, doll." He brings my hand to his lips and kisses my knuckles before releasing my fingers one by one. I'm stuck to him like glue. I don't want to let go.

Two months. I can wait two months. I've been waiting an entire year, so what's a little longer? I follow behind him, and one fistful of clay after the other, I slide down the other side on my butt, dirtying my pants.

Tool is still waiting on the porch, and he gives a small nod before vanishing through the double saloon doors. As I walk to the clubhouse, I think about my brother's offer of moving away from here. When I'm eighteen and things with Reaper don't move forward, maybe I'll tell my brother I'm ready to leave.

These next two months are going to be hell. I wish I didn't know that Reaper has feelings for me. I thought it would be easier knowing than not, but now it's all I can think about.

Well, I made my bed, now I need to lie in it.

I follow behind Jesse, watching his plump behind sway back and forth. I can't wait until the day I can touch it. Grab it. Hold on to it. Kiss it.

Oh, I am definitely going to kiss it.

Slap it.

Hug it.

Whatever the hell I want to do to it, I'm going to.

Within his limits, of course.

We reemerge into the main room, and a few cut-sluts are there. Millie, a woman I know Jesse has fucked more than once, and I hate her for it. There's Darcy; she's kind of new and has been hanging around Tongue a lot. She thinks she's going to be able to break down the barrier Tongue has around him. The woman doesn't know how to take a hint.

There are Olivia, Jasmine, Candy, and Becks. The only one I like out of any of them is Becks because at least she doesn't throw herself at every guy. She waits for one to come to her. Becks never has to wait long. She's gorgeous, and why she is here whoring herself out when she can have anyone she wants is something I'll never understand.

"Reaper," Millie purrs, cutting him off as he walks where Tool is waiting for him at the bar. "Hey, baby, it's been a long time." Millie's red-painted fingernails dig into the material of his shirt, and I know Jesse can feel the sharp pins of her nails sinking into his skin. Images of them together assault me.

Him fucking her from the back.

Her nails leaving red lines down his back.

His ass flexing with every stroke he gives her.

Her moans.

His moans.

God, the thought of him getting off to her makes me sick. He is much older than me, I know he isn't a saint, but I hate being face to face with his conquests. She's wearing cut-off shorts that stop just above the bottom of her ass and a black tube top. She has on thick eye makeup and lipstick is all over her teeth.

Millie has seen better days.

"Hey, Millie." Jesse actually greets her with me standing right here. I want to wave my arms over my head and shout, *'Hey, remember me!'* but I keep my mouth shut and let whatever is about to happen unfold. Jesse reaches up and wraps his hand around hers that is laying on his chest. He gives her a smile that would give any woman the wrong impression.

"Want to grab a drink, Reap? I've missed you. It's been too long." Her eyes cut to mine, narrowing as if I've stepped onto her territory.

Just as I expect Reaper to say no…

"Sure, Millie. Grab me a beer. I'll be over in a second."

He says yes.

He actually fucking says yes.

She gives me a triumphant look, one with a smug smile as she flicks her hair over her shoulders. Millie saunters to the bar, putting an extra sway to her slender hips. Millie is unimpressive in my opinion, but I guess if a man needs a hole, there is one to be filled here.

"You asshole," I say low enough so no one can hear except Jesse. The words are venomous, a hiss on the tip of my tongue like a snake ready to bite. I'm ready to bite too. Ready to sink my fangs into his neck and poison him with my anger, bitterness, and resentment.

Poison him with the heartache he intoxicates me with every day.

Watch him suffer the way I have over the last year.

Have him be paralyzed with the paralytic he stuns me with every time he walks into a room.

I want to give him a taste of his own medicine.

If only my remedy came in a bottle.

"Don't start something you don't understand, doll." He grabs the side of my arm and shoves me toward the hallway, manhandling me, his hold almost bruising. It's different than the way he touched me when we were in the desert.

I guess that's the difference.

There always has to be a show, some sort of front for him to put on whenever I'm around. Well, I'm done. Maybe I'll take that boy at school up on his offer and go out with him since Jesse wants to fuck anything and everything.

"Let go of me!" I rip my arm out of his hold and stare at his face with watery eyes. "Are you going to fuck her?" The music from the main room starts to shake the walls, and laughter spills into the hallway where we are standing. Even with the loud noise, the silence between us tells me everything I need to know. "You're a liar."

"Let me explain—" He reaches for me, but I jump back, staring at him like I've never seen him before. Do I even know who Reaper is?

"I hate you." I regret the words as soon as they're out of my mouth, but I will never take them back.

"No, you don't," he replies, holding a smoke between his lips as if he doesn't have a care in the world. Is this what I get for loving the President of the Ruthless Kings? To be treated so … ruthlessly?

"I want to, *Reaper*." Right here, right now, I do hate him. I hate him for existing and being the only man I want to love, the only man I want to give myself to. In the desert, he was obviously only saying what he thought I wanted to hear to get me back to the clubhouse. "I want to hate you so much."

"No, you don't." He has the nerve to laugh at me. He blows some out of his nose, reminding me of a fire-breathing dragon, and it swirls up and around his face, masking the face that obviously has two sides to it.

Which side am I finally going to get?

The side I want to hate.

Or the side I want to love?

CHAPTER TWELVE

Reaper

I DID SOMETHING I SHOULDN'T HAVE TRIED TO DO. I FUCKED UP. I made a mistake.

I tried to fuck Millie.

Last night, after Sarah told me she hated me, or wanted to hate me. I already had conflicting emotions when we walked into the clubhouse together after our moment in the desert, and I felt like people *knew*.

I had to cover it up. I had to make it seem like I was just dragging her back home, so I took Millie up on her offer with a drink. I knew where drinks led, and what made it worse was that I did it right in front of Sarah. I deserved to be called an asshole, but Sarah had no idea what she did to me, what I didn't want her to do to me, and that these feelings are fucking inevitable.

It's a lot for a man to even admit to feelings. It's a lot for a man to keep control of those feelings and to not fuck the woman he wants to share those feelings with? It's overwhelming. She doesn't understand that wanting her isn't a good thing. Not yet.

I wanted to erase her from my mind and use another woman to help scrub the need of Sarah off my body.

It was wrong of me to do. I'm not proud of it.

I can say this, though, my dick wouldn't get hard. Millie dry-humped me through my clothes, something I usually fucking love, and it gets me so hard I could pound a three-inch nail into the ground.

Not last night. She tried, and I felt like I was cheating on Sarah. I tossed Millie off me so fast that she had no time to right herself, and she smacked her ass on the floor. She called me a limped-dick motherfucker, only to limp out the door because she hurt her leg on the ground.

Once she was out of sight, my cock got hard because a naked image of Sarah invaded my mind. I had to take a cold shower, think of blood, guts, and carving hearts out of people's chests to not touch myself to the thoughts of her.

I can't.

Fuck, I want to.

"You okay?" Tool says at the table. The brothers are gathered around the table, waiting for the meeting to start. I called for church fifteen minutes ago, even for the two prospects, and now I can't fucking remember why because guilt and shame are eating away at me.

I don't even care that I couldn't get it up for Millie. I'm glad I couldn't. It's the hot and cold treatment I keep giving Sarah. She didn't deserve that, and now I have to make up for it for the rest of my life. And I will, gladly.

"You said there was a meeting with Moretti and that he

received my message?" I snap my gaze from the crown engraved in the middle of the table and level my glare on Tool. "When?"

He smirks, sucking his teeth with his tongue. "Not for another two weeks."

"Bullshit." I slam my fist on the table. "We will raid then."

"You sure you want to do that? We have a lot of business wrapped up in the mafia; if we go south—" Tank starts to say, but Ghost shuts him up by kicking him under the table.

It's dead silence.

Prospects never question the President, only patched-in brothers are allowed to. It isn't often prospects are even allowed to step foot in this room, but with the new threat, I want all brothers and prospects to know what is going on. After this, they probably won't be allowed to come into church until they're patched in.

"Is that right, prospect?" I swivel in my chair and lean back, spreading my legs to get comfortable. "How about you tell me how to run my club?"

Tank shakes his head. "No, sir. No, Mr. President—"

I cackle at being called Mr. President.

"I was just concerned."

"Do you know what happens when a prospect questions me?"

A low thrum of hands on the table begins, sounding a low drum in the air, building the anticipation and punishment. Tank shakes his head. He is a big motherfucker, but a huge softy; all that muscle went to waste if you ask me. He's like the Hulk, never wanting to hulk out.

He's too big to tie up and let the bugs get him for the night.

"Aw, come on, Prez. Give him a slide. He was only saying what we were all thinking," Tool defends the guy, which makes sense since Tool is Tank's sponsor. He has been hanging around the club for years now; only recently did he show interest in prospecting. None of us hesitated to throw him the cut and the prospect patch.

He brought a friend too. His name is Tim, nerdy-looking fella with square glasses and a scrawny frame. The guy looks like he can barely lift twenty pounds, but he wears the cut, and Tool is sponsoring him as well. I learned not to judge a book by its cover long ago. Everyone has something to offer to the club; I'm just waiting to see what Tim can.

"You're replacing the saloon doors with large metal industrial ones today. Do I make myself clear?" I tell Tank. When I meet his eyes, he looks away from me. Submissive, interesting. "Let me tell you something I used to tell Boomer—Always look a man in the eye when he is speaking to you. Don't be a coward."

"Yes, Mr. President, sir. Reaper. Sir."

Good. God. What the fuck happened to this guy? "You too, Tim. You can lift the hammer or something."

He beams as if he just won a million bucks. "You got it, Prez."

"Tool, Bullseye, we are going to see Moretti today."

"Uh, Prez?" Tongue speaks up for the first time all year in church, and it makes me sit back from beating the gavel on the table.

"Yeah, Tongue?"

"We need to talk about what we are going to do for Sarah's birthday. I already got her a fake I.D., but I'm not giving it to her until that day. I thought we could take her out on the strip, show her a good time."

I narrow my eyes at Tongue, wondering if he has a thing

for my girl because he has gotten real talkative when it comes to her. "Her birthday isn't for another month, three weeks, and eighteen hours, Tongue."

A few laughs covered by coughs sound all around, and I realize my slip. I've been counting down, literally, to the hour. "Um, yeah, plan whatever. It's fine." Fuck, I'm so screwed. Everyone knows how I feel about her now. "Dismissed." I slam the gavel down before anyone else can ask me questions about her.

"Tool, before we leave, I want to go see Boomer, and then we will head out. Get the bikes ready." I stride out the door and take a left before anyone can stop me, but as I'm walking down the hall, Sarah comes out of her room wearing a bikini top and short jean shorts. Hell fucking no does she think she is going out in that. I point to her room. "Go change."

"Nope, sorry. I have a date."

The word date has my blood on fire. Instantly, I want to kill the guy.

"Reap!" Tool yells at me from the saloon doors, and his voice easily carries into the kitchen. "We have a guest."

Sarah gives me a look that can only be described as 'go eat shit' and pushes past me. I get a whiff of that peach perfume, and my cock perks up, begging for some type of attention. "I'm going to spank your ass if you even think about walking out those doors."

"Well then, I guess I deserve to nail your balls to the damn wall after what you did last night!" She spins around quick, her hair flying around her and whipping me in the face as a leather whip would.

"You have no idea what happened last night." I hoped.

"Millie's whorish moans could be heard through a burnt

piece of paper. Nice try. I have a date, who is my prom date too. Who knows, maybe I'll give it up to him. I'm tired of waiting around." Sarah tosses her hair up into a messy bun, a few strands falling free to frame her face, and that's when I smell the lemon.

Fuck, she does that when she wants her hair to get blonder. I've seen her a few times, squeezing lemons into a spray bottle, and now I know why. She's going to come back all tan, all blonde, and possibly not innocent.

My chest pumps in shallow beats, and my rage makes my blood speed through my body, clenching my fists. When Sarah tries to open the saloon doors, I hold them shut. Tank is on the other side, holding a drill in the air.

He has a look of pure confusion on his face. "I thought you wanted me to—"

"Shut it, Tank," I say through a nearly wired shut jaw with how tight it is. I swear, I hear my teeth crack in two.

"You aren't having sex with him," I manage to rasp. Red haze falls over my eyes, and my mind is going foggy. I'm about to lose all control, and I can't.

"I can do whatever and whoever the fuck I want." On that note, she pushes against my chest and darts under the saloon doors before I can catch her.

I plow through them, and Tank nearly falls on his ass. I don't stop to check on him. All I see is the silver Lexus convertible waiting in our parking lot. I've never hated a teenage boy before, but I do in that moment.

Sarah runs down the steps with a big smile on her face, throwing herself around the kid in a big hug. She wraps her long legs around him, arms around his neck, and then kisses his cheek.

"Get your fucking hands off her!" I shout and pound down the steps, nearly reaching for my gun. Nearly.

"Reaper." Tool's fingers brush against my cut, almost stopping me by grabbing it, but I'm too quick. "Stop! Shit, shit, shit." I hear him chat behind me as he follows in my footsteps. I can always count on Tool.

The kid drops his hands, and his face pales when he sees me. My large shadow casts over the both of them. I'm nearly an entire foot and a half taller than this asshole driving daddy's car. I place my hands on her hips and pluck her off, dropping her to her feet.

"Reaper," she warns. She never calls me Reaper. I hate it. I want her to call me Jesse again. I'm acting so out of character. I'm usually in control, but Sarah has me messed up eighteen ways to fucking Sunday.

I loom over the mousy brown-headed boy and cross my arms. "Who the fuck are you?"

"I'm—uh—I'm David?" The kid extends his hand to me to introduce himself.

I lift a brow as I stare at his small, childish hand. "You're David? Are you asking me or telling me?"

"Reaper, that's enough."

"I'll fucking say when it's enough!" I shout at her and then take a step closer to the guy who doesn't know his own name.

"Do—don't talk to her—her—like that," he manages to stutter out with red-hot cheeks. He looks like he is about to cry, but you know what? I won't ever admit it, but it takes some balls to do what he just did. I'd respect him any other day if he wasn't trying to take the woman I've been waiting over a year to have.

How are these last few months harder than all the rest?

"Oh, shit," Tool says.

"David, shut up," Sarah warns her little date.

"No, just because he is your ... I don't know, doesn't mean he can treat you like that."

"Boy, do you know who the fuck I am?" I glower, intimidating a kid less than half my size is fucked up. I need to back down, but then I look at Sarah, standing in just jean shorts and a yellow bikini top, and I get fucking angry again.

David's eyes spare a glance at my name tag, and he swallows. He opens his mouth to say something, the boy practically shaking in his tennis shoes, when Sarah gets between us and pokes a finger into my chest, right above my heart, where it has been aching for an entire year.

"You don't get to do this. Not after what you did."

She's right. I don't, but I'm going to anyway. The sadness on her face is what finally has me backing down. She thinks I had sex with Millie, and I'm going to continue to let her think I did.

"Prez, we need to go," Tool reminds me of the meeting for Moretti, and I curse internally. "He will only be there for another hour." Tool is talking about Moretti's casino, well, our casino. I'm not there too much since I let the rest of my brothers handle the security there, but I'm about to pop in. It's never good when the President shows up to things.

"Have her home before dark." I turn toward Sarah, smelling her one last time. Something about this feels off, it doesn't feel right, but I can't stop her from living her life. I've done that too much already. "Have fun, doll." It takes all I have to pull away, but I do, my god, I do. I hop on my hog, crank my bike, and peel out of the parking lot, making sure to send dust and gravel onto the boy's car.

I hope it leaves a mark.

Because I swear, if she comes back anything less than perfect or a hair out of place, I don't care how old he is...

I'll carve his heart out too.

CHAPTER THIRTEEN

Reaper

WE STOP AT HOTEL ROYALE AND PARK OUR BIKES. WHEN the valets see our cuts, they don't bother asking for our keys. We own half this place. Our bikes stay where they are. We walk in, in torn jeans and greased up t-shirts, but it's our cuts that have people turning their heads. I don't care about any of them. I have one man to see.

And I need to know if he is the reason why my kid is laid up in bed healing over a bullet wound. Being here doesn't even take my mind off the fact that Sarah is with another man right now. No, not a man.

A boy.

Someone her age.

A few guards block our paths, and I want to laugh in their faces. Now's not the time to test me. A few customers are look-ing, and the women look nervous. Me and my club revamped this entire place, poured blood, sweat, and more blood into making it ours. The entirety is black tile, black velvet, with red ceilings. Everything beyond is in colored coordination with a royal flush. I'm standing under a chandelier, something that's new, something I sure as hell didn't approve of. This must be all Moretti.

"You don't want to do this, fellas." I open my cut to reveal my Ruger .22 Revolver. It's forty-two ounces of pure fucking mayhem. I love this gun. It doesn't hold many bullets, but I never need a lot. I always aim right for the heart.

And I never miss.

"Is Moretti expecting you?" the guy on the right asks. He looks fresh out of a frat house, and I want nothing more than to show him how things go down in Vegas.

"It's about his son," Tool says, making our arrival sound less threatening. It's why he is my VP. I want to raise hell wherever I go.

One of Moretti's goons speak into his earpiece, and when he receives a response, he parts to let us through. I give him a grin. "Big thanks, fellas." We stroll over to the elevator, and I hit the button with my fist. "They should have let us by. We own half this place. Hell, I have a few men here right now in that private fucking room that's so important for business, probably about to run fucking money across state lines. We should be allowed in here, Tool, without question."

"I'm glad they stopped us because your head isn't in the fucking game." He punches the button to the top floors and the elevator doors slide shut. "Listen, I don't know what the fuck is going on with you and Sarah—"

Sweat and panic cloaks my skin at being found out. "What? Nothing is happening. I'm not fucking her," I repeat, and when I hear myself, I sound like a liar. I don't know what has gotten into me, but he is right—I'm losing it.

The buttons light up as the elevator climbs the floors.

"Listen, it isn't unknown to everyone that something is happening between the two of you. I know you better than to think you are fucking someone underage, but until she is eighteen, get your head on straight."

"I'm trying!" I shout, pounding my chest. "You don't think I'm giving it everything I have? You think I want this? You think I want to want Hawk's fucking daughter? The guilt I feel. It eats me alive. It isn't right. I fought it, but she's the fucking devil, and she keeps pushing me and pushing me."

He gives a tilt of lips and huffs a laugh. "Yeah, she's a little crazy, but I also know she's young and stubborn, temperamental, and feeling something beyond what you are feeling."

"Yeah, like what?"

"First love, Prez. She's crushed right now. You think you have it bad?" He shakes his head. "Man, that girl has been in love with you from day one. Just remember it isn't easy on her. Especially knowing you've been with other women. I can bet that's the only reason she went out with Trust Fund."

"Trust fund?"

"The guy, Danny or Dante."

"David," I mutter.

"Whatever. She is only going out with him to piss you off."

"It's working. I don't know, Tool. I might have you lock me away for a while. You can take the President patch."

He slams his fist on the red button, and the elevator comes to a stop. "What did you just say? Are you really wound that tight? Did Millie not help you out last night?"

"I didn't fuck Millie last night."

"We heard—"

"You heard her trying to... Just forget it, okay?" I press the button to get us going again, not wanting to talk about my lack of erection, and wanting to get this meeting over with.

Tool presses the button again, and I groan when the elevator comes to a stop. This is getting annoying. He narrows his eyes at me, and then they round when the lightbulb flickers on in his head. "Holy shit."

"Shut up."

"You couldn't—"

"I said, shut up."

"Prez..."

I slam the button harder than I need to, and the elevator ascends again. "Like I said—I don't want to talk about it."

"You got it."

I'm not the kind of man to get embarrassed, but right now, my neck is on fire with how hot my face is. I clear my throat when the elevator comes to a stop, and the doors slide open. The office is nice, plain; nothing like downstairs. This office has white walls, marble floors, and lights in the divots above the walls to give it a welcoming glow.

We walk right by the woman, and she gets up in a hurry. "I'm sorry, I'm going to have to call you back." She hangs up the phone and runs after us. "Excuse me! You can't go in there. You need an appointment—"

"Yeah, about those..." I say slowly and kick the door open to find Moretti standing up with a half-naked woman on her knees in between his legs. I kick a half smile on my face when he taps the back of her head.

She stops and glances over her shoulder at us, licking her lips. He stuffs himself inside his pants, and the long-legged brunette does nothing for me as she saunters our way. She has big fake tits, ones that I've seen a hundred times before at the club. It's not impressive to me. Not anymore.

"Sorry to interrupt."

"I doubt you are," Moretti says as he sits in the chair at his desk. The woman leaves, and Tool doesn't even give her a second look. She shuts the door behind her, and Moretti sighs. "I'm glad you interrupted. The bitch can't give good head to save her life."

"You need new bitches," Tool says as we walk to the two chairs in front of Moretti and sit down. "Bitches who can't suck cock, can't take cock."

Moretti seems amused and laces his hands together. "A fine slogan to live by…" Moretti glances at the name on Tool's vest. "Tool. I like you." He shakes his finger at him.

"Sorry, I don't suck cock."

I chuckle. Typical Tool.

"That's too bad, isn't it?" Moretti whips back.

Oh. *Oh!* Now that is unexpected.

"Uh—"

But Moretti cuts Tool off. "I'd do good things to you, Tool. You sure you don't want to take me up on my offer? I'll pay you."

"I'm not a whore you can buy," Tool states with a flush on his cheeks.

Moretti comes around the table, his cock still tenting his pants as he stares at Tool. "That's where you are wrong. Everyone can be bought, Tool. Everyone. Everything." Moretti Spreads his arms, acting as if he is king of the world. Moretti is your typical Italian guy. Olive skin, dark hair, dark green eyes, and has a thick Italian accent. It's like he came in off the damn boat. "What can I do for the Ruthless Kings,

Reaper?" He finally notices me. Jeez, the guy has a serious hard-on for Tool.

I hate to say it, but I might have to use Tool to get closer to Moretti. Orders are orders. This can work out for us.

"I want to know if you sent the hit on my men. I'm here, asking, man to man, not to war; no nothing." I lean back in the chair and get comfortable. "If you lie to me, things change—our truce changes. Everything changes. Our partnership will be dissolved, and you can find your muscle elsewhere, and you'd give me the other half of the casino you own."

"I respect you and your kings greatly, Mr. Reaper."

Tool snorts. Mr. Reaper. That's a new one.

"I didn't send a hit on my most reliable ally."

"A little birdie told me your stepson is estranged, and it could have been him," I say.

Moretti lifts his lips in annoyance, and if I'm not mistaken by the darkened shine to his eyes, hatred. "The little birdie you had delivered on my doorstep. Do you know how long it took to get the smell off my porch? Disgusting."

"I wanted to relay a message."

"Message fucking relayed." Moretti glances out the large windows that take up the entire wall behind him and stares over the view of the city. The Bellagio is right in front of him, and the water show is currently going on. Even from where I sit, I see the different colored lights glow against the sky as the sun sets. "It's not me. You have my everlasting allegiance. We will make a contract if you want. I didn't do this to you, but if it was my stepson, I'm sorry to say, I do not know where he is. He stole from me and vanished. I've been searching for him. I hate the little fucker."

"If I find out you're protecting him—"

"Then you can have the casino, Mr. Reaper. I do not break my truces. Your club is good for me. My men are good for your club."

"I'm going to suspect something big is coming. Anything you hear, tell me, and I'll do the same for you."

He holds out his hand to make it a gentlemen's deal. "Please, I would not have it any other way."

I stare at his perfectly manicured hand and slap my grease-stained, calloused one against his palm. "Thanks for your time, and sorry for the interruption."

He smirks and places his eyes on Tool, holding out his hand for my VP to take. It isn't often I see Tool flustered, but he is right now. Tool places his hand in Moretti's, and Moretti jerks Tool forward over the desk.

Damn, the guy is way stronger than he looks.

"Are you sure you don't suck cock?" Moretti asks, a little too close to Tool's lips for Tool's liking.

"I'm positive. Sorry to disappoint, Moretti."

Moretti closes his eyes, shivering from the way Tool says his name. "It is a disappointment, but I understand." Moretti lets go, and Tool takes a gigantic step back, as far away from Moretti as he can get without being disrespectful. "I'll see you guys around, I'm sure."

"Keep in touch," I say as we turn our backs to leave. I hate turning my back. You never know what the person behind you will do. Trust in truce is a difficult concept for me to swallow, but when we make it out the doors, down the elevator, and to our bikes, I wonder if Moretti is really a man of his word.

"How you holding up?" I place my helmet on my head, snapping it under my chin as I give Tool a jab.

"Shut the fuck up," he mutters. "Don't you have your own shit to worry about?"

Right.

My own shit.

For a second, I forgot all about Sarah, and now I'm going home, and she won't be there.

Her birthday needs to hurry the hell up before I go clinically insane.

Shit, I'm already there.

CHAPTER FOURTEEN

Sarah

IT'S PROM NIGHT.

David will be here in an hour, and I'm nowhere near ready.

Everyone here thinks David and I are dating, but no one knows that David is gay, and I plan to keep that my little secret. It's been almost a month and a half since Reaper and I spoke. I actually haven't been here much; I've been hanging out with my new friend. Knowing Reaper is at the clubhouse, fucking some biker slut, it hurts too much.

I have two weeks until graduation.

And then one week after that I turn eighteen, and I already plan on leaving. Being here without being Reaper's, I can't do it. I'm not strong enough.

"Knock, knock."

"Boomer," I say with a large smile on my face when he

enters my room. He is finally up and walking around, but he is slower than he was before. I'm just glad he is out of bed.

"Look at your hair." He boings a curl hanging lose on the side of my face. "It looks good. You look beautiful," he says, and he cups my jaw with his hand. When he looks at me, I know he is my brother, but all I see is our father trying to talk to me right now. "I'm so fucking happy to see you go to prom. It means so much to me. You have no idea how much I love you, Sarah."

My chin wobbles as my eyes fill with tears. "I love you too."

"You really have no idea how important you are to me." He holds a hand to his wound and wobbles on his feet.

"Boomer!" I run to his side before he falls and sit him on the bed. "Don't push yourself."

"No, you need to hear this." He takes my hand in his and holds onto me tight, like he is never going to see me again.

"You're scaring me," I say as a tear falls. "You're going to make me mess up my makeup."

He flashes the same grin that our father has in the photo that I carried with me when I was growing up. "Don't be scared. I just want to say this to you. I don't know. It feels monumental to witness you in a dress, makeup, and hair done. You're all grown up now; you don't need me."

I sit next to him and squeeze his hands. "Is that what you think? Boomer, I'll always need you. I had no idea how much until the day I showed up here. You're my family. I love you more than anything."

"That's good." He coughs, his voice is broken and high-pitched, and that's when I see the tears swimming his eyes. He tilts his head back and looks up at the ceiling. "Shit, I'm such a bitch."

"Shut up." I nudge him with my shoulder. "I love you too. My life wouldn't be what it is if it wasn't for you."

"Your date is here!" Poodle shouts from the main room.

"Oh gosh!" I stand and run my hand down my dress. It's already been an hour? Since when? "Do I look okay?" I glance up at Boomer who stares at me with nothing but brotherly love.

"You're going to be the prettiest woman there, Sarah." He brings our hands above my head and spins me around. The tulle of my yellow dress flows around me, and I smile, actually excited to go to prom.

"Escort me out?"

He holds out his elbow, standing as straight as he can without causing himself pain. "Like I'd have it any other way."

We walk slow, passing my bed, vanity, and bathroom. When we get to the door, Boomer opens it with his free hand, and what I see makes me gasp. All the guys line the hallways on either side of the door. Their beards are combed, their hair is tied back, and they're wearing their best clothes. All of them are in blazers, and they have flowers on the lapels of their suits.

"What…What is all this?" I ask as Boomer takes a step forward between the two lines.

"I asked all the guys to clean up. This is your night. You're the only important woman here in the entire club, Sarah. We wanted to show you that we care about you."

"I'm not getting married." I feel like I'm walking down the aisle.

"Not yet, but whenever you do, we will all be here," Boomer says.

I'm nervous. He says all the men, and I can't help but wonder if that includes Reaper. When I see Tongue on my left, I squeal and throw my arms around his neck. He lifts me into the air, holding me tight. "Look at you! You look gorgeous, Sarah. I got you something," he whispers into my ear as he places me on the floor.

He's careful, since I'm in five-inch heels, and holds me steady. He slips something into my hand and brings his fingers to his lips.

When I take a peek at what it is, I see that it's a fake I.D. I can't help but do a little happy dance and throw my arms around him again. "You're the best! Thank you!"

"Eighteenth birthday, you and me, the strip?"

"Like I'd ever miss it!" I tell him. Gosh, I'm smiling so hard, my cheeks hurt.

"Go, you're going to be late."

I love how slow Tongue talks. People blame it on his accent, but I think it's something else, something deeper; another reason why he doesn't talk much and why he cuts tongues out of others. I just want to know what it is.

I slip my new I.D. in my strapless bra and continue down the makeshift aisle. It's hard to not cry. These men have surrounded me for the last few years, helping me, especially when I needed it most, and it's emotional seeing them all around me, prevailing for me.

Eric finally comes to view. The doctor. The reason why I'm here in the first place. It's hard to keep a straight face because my emotions break when I walk into his chest and lay my head there, letting him hold me softly. "Thank you," I tell him, a tear escaping me. I tried not to cry, but a woman can only hold back so much with all this support surrounding her.

"Aw, sweetheart, no need to thank me. Be safe, okay?" Eric has no idea how much he changed my life the day he found me outside. It all started with him.

I get to the end of the aisle before the new doors. They are metal and have a small square space in the middle that opens for us to look out of. Reaper is serious about safety, but he obviously doesn't care about seeing me out for prom like the others. The guys really set the standard high for any other men. I'm a lucky girl.

Boomer opens the door, and all I see is a massive chest wearing a tux. Slowly, I slide my eyes open until I'm met with Reaper's face. Like the other brothers, his shaggy hair is slicked back. I've never seen him look so uncomfortable.

"You look lovely," he says, lifting his eyes to someone behind me. It's like he is reading off a prompt. "I hope you have a great time tonight. Here, I got this for you."

He sounds weird. Is he actually reading off prompt cards? I try to turn around, but someone's hands on my shoulders stop me. *Okay, I get the picture.* I take the blue velvet box from his palm and open it, gasping when I see the teardrop diamond hanging from a rose gold necklace. "This is beautiful," I say.

"Not as beautiful as you look tonight. It's from all of us." Reaper takes the necklace out of the velvet box, and it looks so fragile in his sausage fingers. I turn around, and he places the necklace around my neck, clasping it. "We love you. Stay safe and call us if you need us." He opens the door, and a long black limo awaits. David is hanging out of the sunroof, shaking a few liquor bottles in the air.

"They're awesoooome!" he shouts, already slurring his words.

"I might have gotten a limo with a full mini-bar, but I didn't think he would drink it all already," Reaper mutters.

I lay my hand on his bicep, his strong, thick muscle, and

feel my lower belly flutter. My heart aches, and I let my hand fall to my side. "He's a lightweight."

"That explains it," he says, rocking on his heels. "I'd like all of us to get a picture. It isn't often our favorite girl goes to prom."

"David?" I shout. "Come take a photo."

He falls out of the car and grins, a flush over his cheeks from the alcohol. "You got it."

I hand over my phone and all twenty or so brothers line up on the porch. I stand between Reaper, Boomer, and Tongue, and grin. The flash of the photo blinds me for a second, and before my eyes can readjust, he takes another picture, and another.

Reaper lifts me up into his arms, and he and I stare at one another as the flash goes off. I'm not too sure what his eyes are saying, but I know my heart is screaming for us to be together at last.

He sets me down carefully, making sure to keep ahold of the back of my train so I don't step on it with my heels. "You're going to have the night of your life," he says.

I know that the best night of my life will be the one I have with Reaper if he and I can ever get over our differences. I make my way down the steps, but Reaper grabs ahold of my hand, stopping me in my tracks.

I glance over my shoulder to look at him and then back at David who is waiting for me to get in the car. "I'll be there in a second!" I raise my voice a bit so David can hear me, and he climbs in the limo, keeping the door open.

The brothers head inside the clubhouse, leaving me alone with Reaper.

It's just the two of us under the night of the sky, the stars twinkling with every blink of our eyes. It's romantic with the sound of crickets and frogs singing all around us. I want to dance with him, lay my hands on his shoulders while his fall at my waist, as I sink into him.

Instead, I keep my distance because I know where I stand with him now.

"Stay safe tonight, okay? If anything happens, if you need me, I want you to call me or any of the guys, and we will come as soon as possible, do you understand? Anything at all, Sarah; I mean it."

I nod with understanding. "I'll call Boomer if I feel the need to; don't worry."

I see the hurt across his face, like I've slapped him or something. He clears his throat, glancing down at the space between us. I guess it's just like our age difference.

It's there when it doesn't need to be.

"You can call me too," he says. "You know I'll always be there."

"I know, but I think it's best if I don't call you, Reaper. I'm trying to give you what you want. You can be with whoever you want, okay? I'm stepping back. I'm moving on." I'm not moving on, but I don't want him to know that. A man his age, his caliber, he deserves to grip life, or ass, with his hands.

And if ass is what he wants, who I am to get into his way?

"It isn't like that, Sarah."

"What's it like, then?"

"Go." He juts his chin toward the limo. "Let's not talk about it tonight. Go have fun and if…" His Adam's apple bobs, and he struggles to form the words. "If you and David do more than dance, just be safe."

Before I muster a laugh, he spins on his heel and heads inside, leaving me stunned and a little grossed out at the thought of David and me having sex.

I stare at his retreating form too fondly before walking down the steps and sliding into the limo. "Let me see the phone," I tell David, and he drunkenly hands it over to me, falling on the floor of the car, giggling.

The first picture that comes up is the one of me and the entire crew. My family. I flip to find my favorite one, but I can't decide. It's so amazing that someone like me has the support and love out of a motorcycle club like the notorious Ruthless Kings. I keep flipping through photos until the one of Reaper holding me comes to view.

Everyone else is staring at the camera, but Reaper and I are locked onto one another. My hand is on his chest, and as I zoom in, I see the look of love shining off my face as I look into his chocolate eyes that almost blend into the night.

Curious, I zoom in on his face, and a flame of hope ignites in my chest. The way he is looking at me, that isn't a look of a man who hates or despises me.

That's a look of a man who loves me.

"Come on! Let's go to prom!" David shouts as he peeks his head through the sunroof. "I'm going to dance my ass off."

"Are you even going to make it to prom?" I question him with a sly grin and send the pictures to myself from David's phone.

"Of course, I am. I'm going to be the life of the party," he slurs, matter of factually.

That I do not doubt.

It's one of the best nights of my life. Things may be strained between Reaper and me, but I know I'll never be able to thank him enough for giving me a life I thought I'd only ever have when I died at the hands of my foster dad.

I'm going to prom!

I never thought I'd live to see the day.

CHAPTER FIFTEEN

Reaper

PROM WAS HARD.

I stayed up all night until she walked through the door, and only then could I sleep. They wouldn't let me be a chaperone. I had asked months in advance, but they didn't want the kids to be scared. Scared! What the fuck would I ever do to a kid? So I had to wait like a good boy until she got home. And I couldn't help but wonder if she had lost her virginity to that asshole David. I shouldn't be thinking about that at all, but I am because it was meant to be mine.

Graduation?

That was easy. I was so proud of her for walking across that stage after everything she has been through. It was a day she rightfully deserved.

The biggest day of my life is in one day. Her birthday.

Sarah will finally be eighteen, and I can't fucking wait to be able to breathe again. I haven't been able to take a full breath since the moment she stumbled into my life. I feel like I've been drunk for a week straight with all the damn events happening. We've celebrated every day and tonight, at midnight, we are hitting the strip to make sure she has a day she can remember.

Right now, she is getting her hair done, and the only thing I can think about is *what if she ruins her beautiful blonde hair?*

"Squeeze that bottle any tighter, you're going to break it," Tool says as he takes the stool next to me.

I grunt in response, bringing the longneck to my mouth and letting the bitter taste of it coat my throat. It isn't enough to wash down the anticipation of what could happen at midnight. I've had this idea in my head for a while now that once that clock strikes midnight, I'll sweep her off her feet and finally take that kiss I've been dying for.

I glance at my watch and groan. It's only been two minutes since the last time I checked.

"Waiting for something?" Tool's grin says it all. He knows why I'm so fidgety and anxious. Sarah and I haven't been on the best terms lately, and every single day that passes, the tension only becomes thicker and more difficult to manage.

"I'm really not in the mood for small talk, Tool. I'm really not. It's been a tough week. I'll just be glad when it's over." Because when it's over, it means I'm sliding into her virgin cunt and claiming it as mine.

"I just bet you are."

"Stop your cheekiness. This isn't funny," I grumble.

"Okay—" Tongue slaps a piece of paper in front of me, causing the bottle to slide from my lips and spill all over me.

"Shit, Tongue! Damn it," I shake off the liquid from my shirt, and a few drops get on the paper in front of me. "What's this?"

"Sorry, Prez," he says real slow like. Tongue reaches in his back pocket and tugs a blade out of his jeans and glides it along his skin, as if it is second nature. "It's just the plan for Sarah's birthday. What do you think?"

I stop shaking my shirt off and lift a brow at Tongue, impressed and a bit jealous he would come up with a schedule. I thought we would hit one side of the strip and then the other, and just see where the night takes us. Apparently, I'm an asshole because women like the big party sort of thing—the plan, the cake, the giggles—all that bullshit, and I was just going to let her hop around.

Jesus Christ. I know nothing.

"That's a gay bar." I point to the sheet. "Why would she want to go there?"

"She told me she wanted to go to one."

"Do you guys have late night pillow-talks or some shit? How do you know her so fucking well?" Jealousy eats at me. I barely put in any effort to get to know her over the last few months. It became too hard, too unbearable not to do more than to just talk to her, but I don't like one of my own men sneaking behind my back and trying to win her over. Everyone here knows she's mine.

And everyone fucking knows I've been waiting for the time to come to make her my ol' lady.

"We hang out."

That gets me out of my chair in no time. I have him pressed against the bar, arm against his throat, and my other hand has ahold of his wrist so he can't swipe me with that knife. I know better than to think Tongue won't attack me. There's something broken inside the man, something sick, and President or not, he doesn't care—if he is threatened, he will retaliate.

119

His eyes swirl with lightning, brewing that psychotic storm I know is inside him. "You hang out? Is that all you do? What are you doing hanging out with her? Tell me the truth?" I slam him down on the bar, and Tool pushes me off Tongue, blocking me from him.

"You're making a damn scene," Tool says. "Walk it off."

"Fuck you. I'm not going anywhere until I get an answer from him." I toss my beer bottle over my head, throwing it right next to Tongue's head. He doesn't flinch. Poodle is behind the bar, and he ducks down just in time before the bottle lands directly in the middle of the liquor shelves.

Glass shatters as a hundred bourbon, rum, vodka, gin, and every other liquor bottle falls to the ground. Thousands of dollars ruined on the floor. No one says a word. Drips of alcohol and weak glass fall, but everyone's attention is on me. None of this would have happened if I turned her away when she came here. I should have turned her away, but one look into those brown eyes, and I fucking knew I was a goner.

And she has gone and ruined fucking everything. My life has completely changed.

"I hang out with her because we are friends, not that you deserve an answer." Tongue tilts his head, and he looks like he is about to slit my throat with the murderous glare he has in his eyes.

I launch myself at him, but Tool blocks me again and pushes me so hard, I slam against the wall. "Go fucking take a walk, Reaper. Go to the garage. Get some air."

"I'll do whatever the f—"

"I'm calling a vote if you don't."

"You're challenging me?" A satanic laugh boils from my throat. "You have to be fucking kidding me. Fuck all of you.

I'm out." Something about the way all of them looked at me made me feel weak, broken, like I'm not fit for my patch. It pisses me off. I brush by Tank and Skirt, Poodle and his goddamn sissy dog, and make my way toward my bike.

I need fresh air, Tool is right about that, and riding on my bike is just what I need. I swing my leg over the seat, it's warm from the sun, and crank the powerful engine. It rumbles, and automatically I feel better. Most of the anger leaves me, but I feel it, simmering and waiting to boil over.

I'm a quick pull of the trigger right now, and it's best if everyone stays out of my way. My phone rings just as I'm about to pull away, and I pick it up on the first ring. "What?" I snap.

"I have a job for you. It's last minute. I need it done. Now. Can you do it?" Moretti asks, his tone calm and cool. He doesn't sound urgent at all, but for him to make a call to me, that tells me it's important that it gets done.

"Sure. I'll be there in ten." I usually always take my men with me, always Tool and Bullseye. They're my righthand men. After what just happened in there, I need some space, and this run is exactly what I need.

I shove my phone in my cut pocket and speed out of the parking lot. I roll down the pavement, the heat waving through the air is so damn hot, and the buildings in the distance look like a mirage. I place one hand on my thigh and keep the other one on the handlebar, enjoying the fucking peace and freedom the road brings.

I'm not sure when my life got so hard. I thought all the hard shit was over. I didn't know I'd constantly have my strength and will tested over a woman, and not just any woman. Sarah. Out of all the runs, the drugs, the weapons, the gambling, the everything else that I shouldn't have done, but I do anyway list, I still can't see myself putting her on that list.

I push her to the back of my mind and roar down the road, enjoying the wind in my hair as I get closer to the city. I'll do this one job and make it back in time for her party. And then maybe after waiting for so long, I'll admit my feelings to her, and we can live happily ever after at last.

When I pull up to the hotel, an uneasy feeling creeps into my body. There's no one going in and no one coming out, which is odd for a place like Vegas. People are always gambling, always casino hopping, and always looking for a good time. I swing my leg over to get off the bike when I get another call. When I look at the screen, it's a text from Moretti telling me not to come in, that it's a trap. Moretti's stepson is there.

I press the call button, and a large blast blares through the lobby of the casino. It's large enough and strong enough to lift my bike off the ground and slam it directly into my body. I fly back as fire lights up the sky, searing parts of my skin. I scream in agony as my skin blisters along my arms. My back hits the ground, my shirt ripping against the pavement and my skin peeling along with it. My bike hits against my stomach, landing on me and keeping me pinned to the ground.

I try to get up, but the only thing I see is black smoke rolling out of the hotel like thunderous clouds. Orange and yellow flames lick the sky. My vision blurs as I try to hold onto consciousness, but no one is coming out of that hotel. No one.

Is Moretti okay? This had to be a set up for me and my brothers. It's the only thing that can be explained. That means Moretti has to be behind the shooting of Boomer. If I make it out of this and if Moretti isn't dead, he and his stepson will be. It makes no sense for Moretti to ask me to go on a run and then blow the fucking business to the ground. Something fishy is going on here. Fuck, I really wanted that truce with Moretti.

Sirens wail in the distance, and the ringing sound bounces inside my throbbing skull. Every inch of me hurts. "Sarah," I say on a struggled breath.

"Sir? Can you hear me? Who is Sarah?" A paramedic shines a fucking light in my eye, and I knock the flashlight out of his hand.

"Ow, motherfucker. I just got blown up; have some damn sense," I wheeze and cough, blood filling my throat. Fuck, it's getting really hard to breathe.

"His pressure is dropping; we really need to get him to the hospital."

The last thing I remember is thinking about Sarah. There's no way I'm making it to her party now. I wonder if I'll be out of the hospital before midnight.

Tonight is supposed to be the most important night of my life. "I'm sorry," I mumble. "I'm so sorry."

"You're going to be okay, sir. Don't apologize."

Sarah.

CHAPTER SIXTEEN

Sarah

THE CLOCK HAS OFFICIALLY STRUCK MIDNIGHT, AND REAPER IS nowhere to be found. To say I'm disappointed is an understatement. I'm devastated. Any hope I had for us is gone. All the guys are in the main room of the clubhouse, ready to go out, even Boomer, but no one can get ahold of Reaper.

Tongue pushes his way through the crowd, and he gives me a tight smile, one that's filled with bad news, I assume. I fidget, rubbing my hands down my new dress. It has a leather bodice and laces up the back like a corset. The bottom is flowy and lands just above my mid-thigh. My blonde hair is platinum now and in long waves cascading down my back. I'm wearing the cherry lip-gloss I know Reaper loves so much.

I'm all dressed up and no Reaper to impress.

All this effort for nothing. I don't even want to go out

anymore. I just want to lay in bed, put on sad, sappy music, and cry myself to sleep like the hopeless, love-drunk fool I am.

"He'll be here," Tongue says as he stops in front of me. I know he is only saying that to make me feel better because everyone knows that Reaper's not going to be here, or he would be here already.

I'm eighteen, according to the clock.

Something I thought Reaper and I were both counting down.

Tongue slides his hand around my shoulders and tucks me into his chest. "It'll be alright." Tongue has become my best friend here, other than my brother, and it's a big deal. I don't take his friendship for granted. Tongue doesn't get close to people, he doesn't talk much, and there is a reason for that; something he has trusted me with. I'll take to my grave what he told me because it seems like the only other person I can trust here besides Boomer is Tongue.

"I thought it would be different. I thought—"

"I know. All of us did too." He kisses the top of my head, and tears burn the back of my eyes. If Reaper wanted to rip my heart out, all he had to do was tell me. Ghosting hurts so much worse. People sometimes beg for others to talk to them, but not me; I know when someone is speaking with their actions.

And Reaper is shouting it loud and fucking clear.

A loud whistle rips through the air, and the heavy metal blaring from the jukebox dies down. A low murmur runs through the crowd, and Poodle stands next to me, handing me a drink. It's a beer. I wanted to go out tonight and try some new fruity drinks since all they have here is whiskey and beer, but I guess that isn't happening.

"Excuse me!" Boomer stands on the table with his arm

wrapped around Candy's waist. Yuck. He can do so much better than that.

Everyone gives their attention to him; a swarm of black leather cuts stand still at attention. Boomer isn't part of the club yet. He is family, but he hasn't really brought it up. Everyone thought he would be a shoo-in. Boomer is a hard read. Some days, he is all about it, and others he hates it.

"Tonight is all about my baby sister, Sarah!"

"Ahooo!"

"Arf, Arf, Arf!"

All the guys make loud cheering sounds and barking noises as they stomp on the wooden planks. My entire body shakes from the force, and I giggle, smiling for the first time all night.

"Sarah!" He lifts his drink, and his eyes land on mine through the crowd. I'm all the way in the back, but he always manages to find me quickly. "The last two years have been a ride. You're an adult now, and I can't control what you do, but I can promise this—I'll always protect you. You came into my life when I needed you most. Tonight, we celebrate you. Happy birthday, kid. I love you. Here's to a good fucking night!" he roars, lifting his drink in the air as the men continue to stomp, and we all down our beers.

It's a stampede of animals through here.

Tool comes up to me next, takes my hand, and spins me around. "Why, aren't you just a vision? You ready to go?"

"We're still going?" I spin by Tongue before facing Tool again.

"Why wouldn't we? It's your birthday! Tongue has planned the entire night, so suck it up. You're stuck with all of us bikers."

I throw my arms around him, giving him a tight hug. My fingers don't even touch behind his back. "Thank you."

"He's a fool, you know. He left all pissed off earlier because of Tongue here."

I want to know what happened, but I don't have the energy or want to care right now. I want to move on with my life, with my night, and celebrate that I'm an adult. Maybe I'll make out with someone tonight. Maybe I'll have sex. I hope it's a night full of firsts because I'm done waiting.

"Hey! Turn it down. I'm getting a call," Tool's voice bellows over everyone and the blaring unclean vocals bursting through the speakers. Everyone still drinks and continues partying.

Becks is trying to talk to shy Tank, but I don't see her getting anywhere with that. I keep looking around and see Badge, the cop who is usually never around, scanning the place. He knows I'm underage, but he is here to celebrate with me. He has to pick and choose his battles, and I'm glad he decided to look the other way for me tonight.

Pirate is in another corner, a bottle of rum in one hand and his other on the back of a woman's head that I don't recognize as she sucks his cock. She's on her knees and fingering herself as she gives him head.

I want to give someone head.

I want to fuck someone.

This entire place is full of sex, alcohol, and whatever else that's good for the soul, and I haven't been able to experience any of it. And seeing it all around is doing this to my body, and I want Reaper. I don't want slow. I don't want tender.

I want hard.

Fast.

Raw.

Primal.

I want everything I know Reaper is.

"Who was it?" Tongue asks Tool when he comes back inside from his phone call.

"I don't know. They kept breaking up. They sounded out of breath."

"Is it Reaper? Is he okay?" I step forward and analyze Tool's facial expression. I can't tell if he is worried or not.

"I think it was a butt dial, to be honest." He tucks his phone in his pocket and glances at his watch. "Sin City is at its peak right now. You ready, blondie?"

It feels wrong going out without Reaper. I don't know. Something is off; something doesn't feel right. There is a twist in my stomach, and my instincts are telling me that while Reaper and I have been on thin ice, he wouldn't have missed this for the world. "How long has he been gone?" I switch my gaze from Tool to Tongue. When they share an unsure glance, my patience snaps. "How long!" I scream, and that gets everyone's attention. The music is off, and the conversation has died down to nothing but a whisper.

"Sarah—"

"How fucking long, Tool?"

"What's going on?" my brother asks from behind me.

I point to the VP. "They won't tell me how long Reaper has been gone."

"He's probably blowing off steam, fucking some skirt. Don't worry about it."

I wince. Boomer couldn't have slapped me harder if he tried. "Sorry, Sarah. It's true. You don't know the man."

"What the fuck is your problem?" Tool picks up Boomer by a thin thread of his shirt and slams him against the wall. "What the hell have we done to you?"

Boomer leans forward and curls his lip. "I think the better question is, what haven't you done?"

"You mother—" Tool rears his fist back to punch Boomer, but I duck under Tool's muscular arm, blocking his attack. He doesn't have time to stop. He fists slams against my cheek, and I crumble to the ground. My head spins, and my vision blurs. Holy shit, I think I see stars.

"Sarah!" Boomer, Tool, and Tongue say in unison as they all drop to their knees to check on me. "Shit, you crazy bitch. What the fuck were you thinking?" Tongue turns my cheek to see the damage. "Reaper is going to kill you, Tool."

"Fuck, he is going to have my patch. I'm screwed. I hurt his ol' lady. Are you okay, Sarah?"

I groan, and Boomer lifts me up into his arm, settling half my body into his lap. "Ouch!" I go to touch my jaw, but wince when my finger grazes it. "That hurt."

"No shit, getting hit by Tool is like getting hit by a truck. We need to take you to the hospital," Boomer states and tries to pick me up, but he drops to his knees and struggles to catch his breath. "Just give me a second." He is still healing from the gunshot wound, and the recovery is slow. He doesn't need to be picking me up anyway.

"I'm fine. It's just a scratch."

"A scratch I'm going to get killed for." Tool rubs his face with his hands. He suddenly looks ten years older. I've never seen him scared, but Tool might run for his life. "I'm so sorry, Sarah. I can't believe you took that hit. What were you thinking? He deserved it for disrespecting the MC."

"He's in enough pain. I'll be his champion and volunteer to take his punishment."

"Jesus, you're fucking nuts." Tool lifts me by the elbows

to help me to my feet. I sway a bit, holding my hand to my head.

"So I've heard," I grumble.

"Doc!" Tool yells, and the crowd parts as Eric comes barging through.

"I'm fine." I bat Tool's hand away.

Eric squats down and examines my shiner. "I'll be the judge of that." His eyes lift to Tool. "You're so fucked, man."

Tool has lost all color in his face and nods. "I know, just check on her. God, I hope I didn't break her jaw."

"No, you didn't. You best count your lucky stars. Her jaw must be made of steel to handle a fist like yours." Eric places an ice pack on my cheek and I sigh with relief. The pain is already starting to go numb. "She might have a concussion. I hate to say it, Sarah, but I really don't think you should go out tonight."

"Fuck!" Tool lifts a stool from the ground and tosses it across the room. It shatters into a thousand splinters, and the loud thud causes the throb in my head to pound harder. "Oh my god. I hit her and ruined her birthday. I'm so fucked. I'm a dead man."

"It's fine." I reach up and take his hand in mine. "I don't blame you. It's my fault."

"You're crazy for taking that for me," Boomer says. "I owe you."

"Damn right, you do. I want all the drinks."

"What do you want? It's yours. I'll go now. I'll buy all of it. Oh, fuck me! I'm screwed." Tool is pacing now, tugging on his hair. "I'll get food too. We will have the party here and then we will get a hotel room, all of us, for the weekend when you're better and really experience the city. Damn it! He's going to reap me, Tongue. He is going to fucking reap me for this!"

Tongue doesn't deny it. He actually doesn't say anything to make Tool feel better. I'm not sure what Tool means, but whatever it is, it has him scared shitless.

"Let's go to town and get all the supplies, alright? Everything will work itself out." Tongue opens the door, and a man stumbles through it, falling directly onto Tool's chest.

It's hard to focus, but I manage. The man in question looks horrible. Half of his body is burnt. He is covered in sand, and half of his scalp is raw with no hair, bleeding down his neck. I'm feeling sick again. The smell of burnt flesh creeps its way into my head and stomach, and I bend over, throwing up onto the ground.

Boomer rubs soothing circles against my back, and I take another look at the man and realize he is having trouble speaking. His body is shivering violently. Eric is at his side and has his medical bag open.

"Moretti? What the fuck?" Tool says with shock. "What the hell happened to you?" He holds the man's head gently as he falls to the floor, placing the burnt head on his lap.

"I'm giving you some morphine," Eric tells the man, squeezing the syringe until medicine jets out of the needle, getting rid of all the air bubbles.

"Hotel. Explosion," Moretti struggles to say. "I didn't know where else to go." His eyes start to roll back, but Tool shakes him a bit.

"No, no, you have to tell us what happened."

"Have you not watched the news?" The man tries to smile, but it only makes him cry out in agony. God, the pain he is experiencing makes tears brim my eyes.

No, we haven't watched the news. None of us have. We have been hanging out, cell phones off, just enjoying the day.

"Turn the TV on," Tool barks, and Knives presses the button on the flat-screen TV. Right away, a building from earlier today fills the news and black smoke clouds the blue sky. It turns the beautiful day into stormy chaos. Fire licks every part of the building, and a second later, the building crumbles to the ground.

"Reaper," Moretti gasps. "There. He was there."

"What!" Clarity hits me, and I fall on the floor and crawl to the man. "Where? Is he okay? Where is he?"

Tool's cell phone rings again. "What?" he snaps. "Yeah, this is Logan." He listens to the other line intently. "What? Yes, we are on our way." He hangs up the phone and slides it into his pocket. "Reaper is at the hospital. Eric, you have Moretti?"

"Yeah. I need help taking him downstairs, but once I get him on the bed, he'll be okay." Eric is lying. I see the disbelief. He isn't sure if Moretti will make it or not.

"Tank, Poodle? You stay here. Bullseye, Tongue, Pirate? You're with me. Sarah? You're coming too."

I'm running out the door and hopping on someone's bike, anyone's. I don't care whose. Reaper is hurt, and he needs me. He will be cornered, and he won't be able to run. I hope he is okay, and we aren't too late.

CHAPTER SEVENTEEN

Reaper

"GET OFF ME!" I PUSH THE MALE NURSE AWAY WHEN HE tries to insert another needle into my arm. The last thing I want is to be high. I'm not in that much pain. I can live with a few burns and cuts. I have a woman to see. I can't miss her birthday.

"Sir, you need to remain calm. You were injured in the—"

I reach out and grab the front collar of his scrubs and yank him forward until I know he can smell the fucking beer on my breath from earlier. "In an explosion? I know. I don't want you to touch me. I have somewhere to be."

"You can't leave. You're injured. You have to stay in bed." The little squirrely looking guy tries to wiggle from my hold, but he can't. His Adam's apple bobs. "It's for your own safety."

"For your own safety, I suggest you take this catheter out of my cock before I rip yours from your damn body."

He nods. "I can do that. That I can do. As long as you stay for twenty-four hours."

Oh, he wants to bribe me. Okay. I can play along. "Fine." I release him by shoving him away, and he rubs his neck, taking deep breaths to remind himself that he is alive. I won't be staying for twenty-four hours. Hell, I won't be staying for one hour once this damn thing is out of my dick. I need to get to my woman.

It's been so long, and tonight is supposed to be the night I make things official. Of course, a damn building would explode to stop me. Karma is a bitch. I swear, this is what I get for loving someone way too fucking young for me. I bet Hawk is having a field day in his grave right now, payback for wanting his daughter.

The male nurse takes the intruding tube from my cock, and I can finally breathe. He snaps his gloves off, mumbling something about alpha assholes and closes the door behind him.

"Move, or I swear to god, I'll move you myself."

"Sarah?" I ask to no one else in the room. That sounds just like her.

"Move it or fucking lose it, dude. I've had a rough day, and if you do not let me in there to see him, I will fillet your skin off and feed it to the damn birds!"

Yep. That's her. That's my maniac.

"You people are batshit crazy," the nurse who just left my room says in a high-pitched voice. "He isn't allowed visitors right now. He needs to rest."

Something slams against the door, followed by Sarah's voice again. "You really want to fuck with me while I have three Ruthless Kings behind me?"

That's my girl. I glance at the clock and see it's nearly one in the morning. Shit, it's her birthday. She's eighteen. My cock hardens, and I let it grow to full mast. I can finally think of her without feeling guilty.

"That's what I thought," she mumbles. "I don't want to be interrupted, okay, Tongue?"

"You got it, Sarah."

I watch as the handle turns, my heart thumping in my chest. My heart monitor picks up the change, and I rip the bandages off my chest, grimacing when the sticky pads take some hair with it. Fuck, that almost hurts more than the wounds on my back.

The door finally opens, and her beautiful blonde head is down. She pushes the door shut behind her and a soft click after tells me she has locked the door. She looks up as tears roll down her face, and that's when I see the bruise on her cheek.

"Who the hell did that to you? Was it that punk outside? I'll kill him." I throw my feet over the bed, and Sarah runs over and places her hands on my chest.

Having her hands on me is a dream. I lift my hand to cover hers. At the same time, we release a shaky breath that can only be described as relief. Finally, she can touch me, and I can touch her.

No guilt.

No second thoughts.

No regrets.

Her hand is warm against my chest. Fuck, I've waited my entire life for this moment. It's what it feels like when the woman you love is finally in front of you. There's no more waiting for me. My life is now. She's it.

"Jesse."

The emotion in her voice has me opening my eyes again, and her deep brown eyes stare at me through raging waters. I cup the back of her head with a marred hand and place our foreheads together. "Don't cry, doll. I'm right here. I'm okay. Don't cry."

Her soft hand cups the side of my face that doesn't have superficial scratches, and she shakes her head. "I could kill you for scaring me like that."

"Sounds like you almost killed the nurse."

"He was in my way."

"Crazy," I mumble, my lips inching closer to hers.

"You love it," she replies like she always does.

I nod, and the scent of that cherry gloss has my cock spurting precum underneath this cheap, scratchy hospital gown. "I do, very much."

"Jesse?" my name is a whispered breath across her lips.

I moan. "Hmm?"

"Kiss me."

I'm a grown fucking man, and I've done a lot of bad shit in my life, but I've done a lot of good. I'm not saying I deserve this because no man deserves something as good and as beautiful as Sarah, but I'll pray to whatever god on my knees every night to thank them for giving me the chance to take care of something so fucking precious.

I've imagined this moment a hundred times, and I never thought I'd go slow, but here I am, wanting it to be perfect. I didn't expect to be in a hospital, covered in bandages, so I guess perfection is ruined.

"Jesus, enough waiting—" She fists the gown at my shoulders and pulls me to her, closing the distance between our lips. The first press of her soft clouds has the animal inside me unleashing and bursting from the cage I've kept it in for so long.

I growl, wrapping my arms around her small waist, and pull her to me. One hand travels down to her ass, squeezing the teenage globe in my palm, while the other cups the back of her head, controlling the kiss. I know she doesn't have much experience, and I love it. It's all mine. Her firsts. Every single last one of them.

I shove my tongue between her lips, and the greedy girl sucks it deeper into her mouth, lapping it like it's my cock. Her enthusiasm has me close to the edge, as it should; I've been waiting for too long for this.

Her lips are velvet, so much softer than what she is feeling right now, I'm sure. My scruff is probably scratching against her flawless face, but she seems to like it. Her mouth, her tongue, it's everything I've wanted and more. She lifts one leg and then the other, pulling her dress up as she straddles my lap.

Her heat sears my aching dick, and both my hands fall to her ass. Sarah takes control and rocks against me, moaning into my mouth when the tip of my cock hits against her clit, and she shakes above me.

I'm not stopping. No way in hell. I deepen the kiss and rock with her, barely able to focus, to breathe; she feels so fucking good in my arms. It feels right. I feel whole.

"Jesse," she moans, and Jesus fucking Christ, I've never heard my name sound so damn hot before. It reminds me of the time I held her during her first nightmare, the way she said Reaper like I was her god, her savior. We've come some far, we've waited so long, and now I can hear my name fall of her lips any damn time I want. "Oh, god. You feel so good."

She breaks the kiss and drops her head against my shoulder

as she rocks, using me for her pleasure. And, of course, she smells like peaches. My fucking favorite. It makes me lose a little of the control I had and thrust my hips up.

She's fucking drenched.

I stare down at my cock, and a large wet spot turns the light green material a darker shade. Fuck, it's hot.

"I was so worried about you," she mumbles against my lips between kisses, and she moves her hips back and forth. "You scared me. I had so many thoughts—"

"Nothing could take me away from you." I abuse her lips with mine, applying so much pressure because I can't get enough. I can't seem to get deeper. I fucking need more. It's on the tip of my tongue to tell her I love her, but the environment isn't right for that. It smells like blood and plastic, disinfectant and sick people. She deserves better than that.

She shoves my gown to the side and breaks the kiss to look at my cock. "Oh, wow…" She licks her lips. "I remember seeing it the first time, but I didn't get a good look." She wraps her fist around the thick base, and I snap my head back, groaning loudly from finally having her touch. "So big, baby," she says in awe.

Damn, she knows how to make a man feel good.

She lifts her dress up, and that's when I see the black lace covering her virgin cunt. I see a faint tease of trimmed blonde hair and another thick drop of precum squirts from my slit. Fuck, I'm not going to last.

I caress my hand up her soft, silky legs, traveling higher until I wrap my fingers around the flimsy thong and rip them off. She cries out, and my eyes lock onto her swollen pink clit. Her juices shine against her thighs as if her pussy is crying out for me.

She gives me a firm stroke and holds me still as she lifts into the air. I'm taken aback. "What—what are you doing?" I stumble through the words; my lust-infused brain can barely manage to string together.

"I'm not waiting any longer, Jesse. I'm going to fuck you," Sarah says. "And you're going to fucking like it." She impales herself so fast on my cock I don't have time to think or stop her.

I bust through her virginity, and both of us cry out. Me in pleasure, her in pain.

I growl, a low, violent rumble shaking my chest. "Don't. Fucking. Move." I'm two seconds away from blowing my load inside her virgin cunt. I wrap my hand around her throat and squeeze. "I should pull out and leave you fucking needy for the rest of the night for what you just pulled."

"Tighter," she snarls. "Do it."

I'm not surprised she likes it a little rough. She wouldn't be made for me if she didn't. I tighten my grip until she's gasping. Sarah starts to rock against my cock, and everything inside me breaks. I don't give a fuck about the burns on my arms or the road rash on my back. I pick her up around the waist, and while she's still fucking my cock, I slam her against the door, choking her how she likes.

Barreling into her, I glance down at my blood-covered cock.

Her virgin blood.

I roar with victory, hammering inside my new home. My cock is never going to leave. Ever. I'm going to tie her to me in every way. She'll be my ol' lady, but she'll be my bride too, and she'll have my babies. I'm going to drench her womb with my seed.

Like how it's meant to be.

"Jesse," she gargles, her face turning a bright shade of red from the lack of oxygen. "Fuck, yes. Harder. Give it to me how you've been wanting."

With a snarl, I flip her around, grip her ass, and fuck her unapologetically. I'm hypnotized by how my cock saws in and out of her cunt. Her fists slam against the door, and she screams my name, mouth open wide.

I bet she wishes my cock could fill that hole right now too.

A loud slap fills the room when I spank her ass. She flips her hair to the other shoulder and peers up at me through glowing amber eyes, searing me with their beauty.

"You like this? You like finally having my cock in this teenage cunt? Tell me." I slap her ass again, and she rears up, wraps her arm around my neck, and instinctively I wrap my hand around it again. I kiss the side of her bruised face, making a mental note to figure out the story there.

"I love it. You're so big. You're splitting me open. Fuck, Jesse. I'm going to come. Make me come."

"You're fucking filthy," I slam my face against the door and watch her ass jiggle, thrusting in and out as fast as I can. My balls slap against her slit, and the beginning tremors of her orgasm trickle along the vein of my cock.

Of course, this isn't romantic.

Nothing about us has ever been, but it's fucking real and desperate.

Everything she and I have always been, so this is exactly how it should be.

She bangs her head against the door again, and her pussy clenches around me. She's so hot, and her walls are tight and soft, hugging me and pulling me deeper. The tip of my cock hits her womb, and my head drops to her back. Her skin is sweaty and warm. My tongue twitches for a taste, so I don't deny myself.

I lick from the middle of her spine to the base of her neck. I see the blank canvas of her nape; I know where I want my property tattoo on her. Right there, for everyone to fucking see, and when I'm giving her my dick, I'll be able to see it every time I come inside her.

Marking her as mine.

Claiming her as mine.

Possessing her as mine.

My toes begin to curl when my orgasm threatens. I reach around and slip my hand between her legs, putting pressure against her clit.

She rears back again, her neck still in my palm, and when she cries out, I let go, knowing her orgasm is going to be that much more intense. The muscles spasm along my cock, and Sarah screams until her voice breaks and turns into a harsh rasp.

"Jesse! Jesse, god, yes!" she says so loud there is no doubt the entire hospital can hear.

"Sarah," I whisper into her ear as I come, grunting as every jet of cum splashes against her insides, bare, raw, and no protection. A guttural, satisfied moan escapes me, and the tremors make my body jerk as I thrust into her, three, four, five times, filling her until my cum is rushing down her thighs.

"I never want to leave you," I say, half-dazed, high off my first of many orgasms with my one and only. I don't want to pull out of her. She's so warm and wet, and this way my cum can stay locked in deep.

"I never want you to." She slumps against the door and hums happily. "Finally."

I kiss the back of her neck and grin. "Finally."

K.L. SAVAGE

The door handle jiggles, and I forgot that she locked it. I back up until we are on the bed and pull out of her, both of us groaning from the loss. Cum and blood mark me. When I spread her legs for a quick look, she has white cream leaving her cunt.

Fuck, I want to be inside her again. Right now.

With an annoyed groan, I fix her dress to hide her pussy, my pussy, and pull my gown down, but it's pointless since I'm still hard.

Sarah giggles, biting her thumb as she stares at the tented hospital dress.

"You think that's funny?" I go to tickle her, but the door-knob jiggles again. I snarl with annoyance, and it makes her giggle again. I point at her. "Watch it, or the next time I fuck you, I won't let you come."

She moans, as if she likes the idea of torture.

"Fuck, woman. You're going to be the death of me. I'm too old to feel like this." I reach for the door handle when her words stop me in my tracks.

"You're perfect for me."

I let the words wash over me, waiting for the guilt and re-pulsion to hit me like it used to. I hated that I wanted her before she was eighteen, but our love was made in the stars, something to last forever.

Shit. Now, I'm a goddamn poet. Look at me.

Masking my happiness, I open the door and snap. "What the fuck do you want?" I stare at Tool, and he swallows, glancing away from me shamefully. He never does that. He always meets my eyes. He knows how I feel about that.

"I'm glad you're okay, Reaper, but we really need to head back to the clubhouse. It's Moretti."

REAPER

I shake my head. "He's dead."

"He's very much alive and at the clubhouse."

Holy shit.

Moretti is alive?

CHAPTER EIGHTEEN

Sarah

WHAT WAS TURNING INTO A HORRIBLE NIGHT, ENDED ON A really great, very pleasurable note. Reaper and I finally had sex.

I'm not a virgin any longer.

He has it.

He has claimed it.

I'm his.

I've never been happier. Was it where I thought it would be? No, but it was perfect. Built up sexual tension can only last so long when the wait was finally over.

And it didn't last long at all. When I saw him in that hospital bed, all banged up and just waiting for me, my pussy was ready, I was ready, and I knew that once we were alone in that room, nothing would stop us.

I have a feeling it will always be like that with us. Well,

maybe not until he is better. That's the only thing I feel guilty about. His arms have second-degree burns, and he has road rash on his back. The reason why it took so long for someone to call us is because his cut got ripped from him when he was thrown from the explosion. When they found it after cleaning up the scene, they immediately sent it to the hospital.

They saw the MC patch and wasted no time calling us. The club does a lot of charity work for the hospital and donated a ton of money to the cancer ward, in honor of Slingshot. He beat cancer when he was in his twenties, so about ten years ago. And now the club is very active when it comes to cancer awareness.

They're not all bad, see?

When we get to the clubhouse, Jesse is moving a lot slower now, grunting with nearly every step he takes. Tongue had taken a truck to the hospital since Jesse's bike was ruined from the explosion.

I know Jesse is never going to ask for help, so I rush to his side when we get to the steps and take on some of his weight to help him up.

"How did you get that shiner on you, doll?"

"It was a misunderstanding, that's all. Don't worry about it." Damn, he is heavy. I tighten my arm around his waist, trying to get a grip on his wide muscles, but he's so thick that my fingers keep slipping.

When we get to the porch, he turns my cheek and brushes his finger down it. He glances at all the guys, and when his gaze lands on Tool, Tool does the one thing that gives him away.

He doesn't meet Jesse's eyes.

"Fuck, I'm getting too old for this shit." With more strength and energy than I thought he had, he slams Tool against the metal door and knocks it backward until they fall inside the main room.

"Reaper!" I rush to him, making sure to say his road name in front of the guys. I don't want him to get disrespected. I watch in horror as he wraps his hands around Tool's throat.

Tool doesn't fight back.

"Reaper, stop it! It was an accident." I try to pull him away, but he is too strong and overcome with rage. "Tool! Tell him." The other brothers of the MC surround us, and Boomer is there, trying to pull Jesse off too, but nothing.

Jesse isn't giving up, and he isn't going quietly. "Why the fuck is my ol' lady bruised?"

"It was meant for me!" Boomer says, pushing Jesse off Tool finally. Jesse hits the ground, and I know it hurts because he holds in the pain, pressing his lips in a firm line and then slamming his fist on the floor, shaking with irate, unhinged aggression and agony.

"What?" Jesse's voice is flat and cold.

"The punch, it was meant for me, but she stood in Tool's way, and Tool's fist was already flying through the air," Boomer tries to explain, waving his hands in the air as he tells the story.

Tool is coughing, rolling around to his hands and knees to try to catch his breath. I've never seen a man as big as Tool vulnerable on the ground, but when your throat is in the hands of the MC President, there isn't much you can do besides submit.

"I volunteered. I wanted to take the punishment," I say, touching Jesse's shoulder. "I wanted to take it. Boomer is injured enough."

Jesse cups my face, bringing his lips to my cheek. "You're insane for doing that. Tool has killed people with one hit."

"If I would have known that, I still would have jumped in front of it to protect my brother."

"No." Jesse steps back. "I don't ever want you to threaten your life like that again; do you understand me?" He points at me. "I can't live without you. I finally have you, and I'm not going to have you taken away because Boomer and Tool can't get their shit together." He swings his gaze toward the two men. Tool just now got to his feet, only to almost fall to his knees again from the power and dominance Jesse's presence brings.

Even injured, Jesse isn't a man to be fucked with.

"I want retribution, Tool."

Tool nods. "I understand, Prez. I apologize. I would never hit a woman. I know it's one of our most sacred laws. I feel terrible about it." His eyes shine with regret as he stares at me. "I'm so sorry, Sarah."

"I wanted it. Stop this! No retribution. I challenged it. I'm Boomer's champion. I'm allowed to take his punishment if I see fit."

"And if you were any other member, I'd allow that. But you're not. You're my ol' lady."

"Don't hurt him," I beg quietly. Tears brim my eyes as I plea for Tool's life. "Please."

"I'll be thinking about punishment. I'm too fucking tired to deal with it tonight, and I have a mafia boss to see, I understand?"

Tool clears his throat, his eyes, if I'm not mistaken, have a bit of glisten in them too. "He is downstairs, Prez. Eric can only keep him conscious for a little while longer, and then he will be putting him in a medically-induced coma."

"Can someone please bring me a bottle of whiskey? What

the fuck does a man have to do around here? For fucking sake, I survived an explosion."

I press my hand against Jesse's chest and give him a stern look. "You're being mean."

"It comes with the job."

Tank, the poor guy, nearly trips on his way back from the bar with a new bottle of Jack, and he holds it out with shaky hands. It surprises me because if he wanted to, he could flick Jesse and send him flying.

To put it in perspective, Reaper, my Jesse, is a towering six-feet-four, and Tank is nearly seven-feet-tall with more muscle than three bodybuilders put together. The man has a heart of gold and is soft. I'm not really sure what he is doing in the biker life, but they love him, so he is family and belongs here.

Jesse twists off the cap and chugs a third of the bottle down, and then he hisses from the burn. "Fuck. That's good. Okay, take me to the man."

As we walk, Jesse turns up the bottle of whiskey and then curses. "I need a new fucking cut! I want it two days from now," he shouts from the basement staircase. His hand lands on Tool's chest and gives him a slight push. "I'll deal with you later." Jesse is slowly walking down the steps. His shirt is off, the mean ugly marks on his back are deep, and some are bleeding. The burns on his arms need rebandaging, and I can see his leg is bothering him.

He's in a lot of pain.

"I'll handle him, Tool. Don't worry."

"I deserve it, blondie."

"Tool, you don't. He is in a lot of pain and is being an ass. I'll take care of it."

"And I'll take what he thinks I deserve. I deserve it."
The massive amount of guilt on his shoulders makes Tool
seem smaller than usual. Tool walks away, heading to the
main room where everyone else is. With a sigh, I enter the
basement.

When I get closer, I hear Jesse and Eric arguing.

"Get in the bed, Reaper."

"No. I'm fine."

"You aren't fucking fine. You need at least three days of
bedrest without moving. You can get an infection. You could
die. Your wounds need debriefing and cleaned. Sit the fuck
down, Reaper."

"No. I need to talk to Moretti."

"You can talk to him when you agree to our terms."

"Oh, fuck you, Doc." Jesse takes another gulp of the whiskey and tries to push by him to get to Moretti.

"I agree with him," I say, knowing damn good and well
that it's hard for a biker to disobey his ol' lady. We are the people they kill and die for. Saying no to me, that will never be
a good thing. Jesse stops in his tracks, shoulders sagging, and
drops the bottle on one of the bed trays. "Reaper, you need to
rest. You can lay next to Moretti and ask him questions. Please,
for me?" I rub my hand over his shoulder, the one that isn't
damaged and bleeding. "Please, baby?"

The moment he exhales, I know I've won. It may seem
like a small victory to some, but with a man as powerful as
Jesse, this is a huge feat.

"Only because you asked so nicely."

"You're such a grump." I come to his side and help him
to the edge of the bed where he sits down. The mattress dips,
and the metal holding the mattress up groans and creaks. All

of us stop breathing, watching the bed to see if it breaks from Reaper's weight. He's so fucking big.

Crap. I want him again. Right now. And now's not the time and place.

"First things first, I need to clean the wounds again, alright?"

"Nope," Reaper says, snagging the whiskey bottle off the tray. "I want to talk to Moretti first, and then you can do whatever you want to me." Reaper snorts. "And that was directed to Sarah, Doc. Not you."

"You deal with him. I'm going upstairs for a beer. I'll be back in five minutes. Five, Reaper. That's all you get, and then I'm putting him in a medically-induced coma."

"Five is all I need."

Eric slides the curtain, letting Moretti come to view. I jerk my head away when I see how bad his injuries are. I don't know how he is alive. Half his face is draped in bandages, and his scalp is raw. Even through the white gauze, I can see the blisters and parts of his skull. The slight lingering smell of burnt flesh is in the air, but the ventilation system Doc wanted installed does a great job at circulating the air to keep it fresh.

"Damn, Moretti," Reaper says in sympathetic awe.

Moretti's teeth chatter when he tries to speak, his body unable to regulate the temperature. His nerves are exposed and raw. The pain he must be feeling ... I can't imagine. I hold down the emotion and bile choking my throat, barely, and sit on the bed Reaper will be using in a few minutes.

I can't look at Moretti. It's too much.

"Reaper. I didn't"—he takes a raspy breath—"betray our agreement."

"I need you to tell me what happened. Can you do that?"

Moretti wheezes again, teeth still clanking together like nails in a rust bucket. "My stepson. He said he would kill my daughter if I didn't call you. Natalia is everything to me. I tried to warn you. He is insane—" Moretti coughs, and a horrible, heartbreaking noise leaves him, making me smother my own cry by lifting my hand to my mouth. The man sounds so broken, and I can't help but wonder if death would be friendlier than this. "Only a few of my men are alive. Their home was the hotel. They have nowhere to go."

"We will figure it out," Reaper reassures him.

"You don't understand." The monitors start to go berserk, and when I finally look at Moretti, he has ahold of Reaper's wide wrist, staring at him with one eye, the other covered with bandages. "He is coming after you. He is coming after her—" He starts to violently shake, and his eyes roll to the back of his head.

A bottle crashing from behind me has me jumping, and Eric jumps over the rail, bypassing the last half of the stairs as he runs toward us. Beer hisses and bubbles, spreading over the steps like a virus.

"Reaper! Lay down and get out of my way. You had your minutes. You're in my house now. My territory, President or not, you will listen to me. Sit the fuck down." Doc loses his shit on Jesse.

No one ever does that, but Reaper takes as step back to let the Doc work. He closes the curtain, leaving us blind to what is happening. Reaper wraps his arms around me, spreads his legs, and settles me between them. "He said you were in danger." His finger lazily travels up my arms, and the move is natural, reminding me of a habit. It's something we have never done, but it feels like we have done it a hundred times.

"He said you were too."

"I don't care about me. I care about you." His hands fall to my ass, leaving his palms on each cheek. "I finally have you. I can't lose you now."

"Don't say that. I want you to always care about your life because I need you alive. I never want to lose you. I need you to be smart and get well before you do anything stupid."

"I promise not to *try* to do anything stupid."

I tug on his hair and yank his face forward. The tip of his nose touches mine, and I rub them together. "That doesn't sound too promising."

The curtain finally opens again, and Reaper spins me around until I'm sitting in his lap, his chin on my shoulder. "How is he?"

Eric is sweating, his scrubs have dots of blood, but nothing too worrying, not like the dark circles around his eyes. The man is going to keel over; it's only a matter of time. He rips off his face mask and tosses it. "I don't know. His chances of survival aren't great. This isn't a burn unit, but I can't take him to the hospital because apparently doctors there can't be trusted and will kill him; his words, not mine. Time will tell."

Time is a real fickle bitch, and I really don't like her.

CHAPTER NINETEEN

Reaper

"OW," I grunt as Doc changes my bandages for the third fucking time in a few hours.

He digs the tweezer a bit harder than usual in the burns on my arms. "Stop being such a baby. You're fine."

I mock him as if I'm a child, and Sarah slaps me on the back of the head. "I said be nice," she scolds, even has the nerve to shake a finger at me. I pretend to bite the tip playfully and then kiss it.

Fuck, finally.

She's finally mine. No one knows what it feels like to be in my shoes, to wait as I did for her, to struggle, to hate myself, to love someone I couldn't have. I convinced myself, or I tried to, that being with her meant betraying Hawk, but that's not the case at all. She's safer with me, with this MC, more than anyone else, and I'll die protecting her.

Hawk would know that.

So I stopped feeling guilty about him a while back.

My soul is finally complete, which is ironic since I'm called Reaper, and I like to take souls, but none of them were meant for me. They were, they are, a job. Sarah owns me. She's the keeper of my soul, and I'm not scared one bit to give to her.

Because she handles every dark, jaded, and haunted part of it.

"I need to talk to you," Boomer's voice comes from the bottom of the steps.

I manage to look over and see him standing there, watching Sarah's fingers play on my arm. He glances away, and it's obvious he is pissed because of the tic in his jaw. Doc puts down the tweezers and lays the last bandage over the burn on my arm.

"You have to be fucking kidding me." Boomer marches to the end of the bed, staring at us with disbelief. "You're with him? He is twice your fucking age, Sarah!"

His words are salt in an almost healed wound, making it raw and tender again. I'm not sure if the age gap is something I'll ever get used to. I'm old enough to be her father, but I'll still give her whatever she wants, anything she wants. I love her more than how much I worry about the damn age difference between us, so that is what I'm going to focus on—the love that's bigger than worry and what society thinks.

Damn them.

Sarah's mine, and I'll love her every day until the rest of my life.

"Not here." Sarah presses her hands against his chest. "Not now. We can talk about it later."

"No. We will talk fucking now. I knew it. I knew something was going on between the two of you these last few years."

Sarah shakes her head. "No, Boomer. It isn't like that. Not at all."

I try to sit up, but the wounds on my back sting in protest which makes me stay where I am. "Listen to her, Boomer. I never touched her, not once; I'd never do that. I waited."

"You waited? Oh, that's fucking rich." He tries to push by Sarah, but she blocks him again; she's stronger than she looks, that's for sure.

"I'm going to go," Doc says awkwardly. "Holler if you need me."

I wait until the stomping of boots is at the top and the door closes, so I know we are alone. "What do you want from me? I waited. She's eighteen—"

"Right, she's only eighteen. Hasn't been eighteen for two days. Waited." He shakes his head.

"I fucking waited as long as I could!" I roar so loud my chest starts to ache. I put my hand over my heart, where Doc took out a piece of steel from my bike that almost punctured my heart. "I waited." I'm seething at this point. No one understands the agony I felt. It was more than the pain I feel right now. "I waited until the moment I could touch her and not a second later."

He launches for me, but Sarah blocks him again with her small body. "I trusted you, and you do this!"

"He did nothing wrong," Sarah says. "Boomer, please. I love him, okay? I love him."

My heart monitor jumps when I hear the words. They stun me, and while I've known for a few years that she liked me, I always thought it was a crush, but love? To have my feelings returned... It's more than I ever dreamed of.

Boomer holds her shoulders and dips his head to meet her

eyes. "You don't know what love is, Sarah. You're too young. He will hurt you. That's what he does. He doesn't know anything else."

"What? That's what you think of me?" His words make me feel like I'm dying all over again. "Was life here with me that bad, Jenkins?" I swallow down the hurt and the emotion. I consider him my son. He may not be blood, but he is the closest thing I've known to having a kid. I drop my head on the pillow and blink away the tears. I'm not a man who cries, but when the man you've helped raise from a boy hates you that fucking much; it's hard not to let it get to you. "I love you, kid. No matter what you think of me."

"Love shouldn't hurt this fucking bad!" He shoves Sarah away, and she yelps, slamming against the corner of the tray. She falls to the floor, and hearing her whimper of pain has me launching off the bed, ripping the IV from my arm.

Blood flies everywhere, and the stitches holding my skin together rip apart. It won't stop me. I grab the end of his shirt, before he can go up the steps, and jerk him back. He crashes against a beam that supports the floor above us, and I wrap my hand around his throat. He claws at my hand, bringing blood to the surface, but he should know by now...

Pain doesn't bother me.

I lift him by the neck, and his feet dangle from the floor. "I'll allow a lot of things, Jenkins. I'll allow you to feel pain, to say what you want to say, to feel how you want to feel about me, but you will not hurt her."

"I didn't mean to. Sarah, I'm sorry!" He kicks to try and get free. "I love you, okay? I'm sorry."

"Put him down," Sarah yells, pulling on my arm to try to get my grip free. "Please, don't hurt him."

I only release him because she tells me to and when he drops to the floor, he coughs so hard he gags, but he doesn't puke.

"If you weren't so important to me, I'd fucking kill you, kid. Do not think about harming my ol' lady."

"Your..." His laugh is sardonic and full of hate. "What can you give her?"

I bend down, my skin splitting more, and blood starts to drip down my body and onto the floor like a broken faucet. "Everything," I break down the word into small syllables so he can understand me. "Fucking. Everything. You should know that."

"Boomer—"

I don't call him Boomer because right now. He doesn't deserve it, but Sarah does. Jenkins struggles to get up and stops her from saying anything further, lifting his hand and silencing her. I don't like anyone silencing her.

"No. I can't... I can't be here knowing you're with him."

"What does that mean?" Sarah sniffles and reaches for her brother, but he moves away, only hurting her further.

Jenkins seems lost, confused, and doesn't take another look at her as he runs up the steps. The last time I saw him look that betrayed was when we buried his father. He trips as he runs up the steps, still not bothering to give us another glance. When the door slams shut, and it's just me and Sarah, my body buckles from the pain, and I fall to my knees.

"Jesse!" She catches me by my side, supports my weight, and grunts as she lifts me up.

"Fuck, that hurts." My head swims, and sweat breaks out all over my body. My feet drag every few steps, and right when I think I'm about to fall over, Sarah lays me on the bed.

"Baby, your back. I'm going to go get Doc, okay?"

"No, you can do it. I don't want anyone else's hands on me. Eric told me you wanted to be a nurse. Now is the time to practice."

"What? After I had training. I don't know what I'm doing, Jesse. I'm not ready for that."

I can hear the tears in her voice still. I reach around and take her hand. "Come here, doll." She trips over herself a few times as she comes in front of me, wiping away those tears that Jenkins caused. That asshole. I want my hands around his throat all over again.

"It's going to be okay, you know."

"How do you know?" she asks.

"Because I love you, doll."

She inhales a sharp breath, and her tears dry up instantly. Her lips are puffy from the salt and look a bit raw, just like when I get done kissing her. "You love me?"

A hot burn slithers up my spine from my wounds being open again. I still manage a smile and bring her knuckles to my lips. "How could I not love you? You think these last few years have been easy? I'm so much older than you. You had no idea how it felt having to wait for you to turn eighteen. Staying away, being rude, fighting you. It was the only way for me to stay sane. It hasn't—" I close my eyes when another round of pain hits. "It hasn't been easy, and I can't promise it will always be a smooth ride, but I promise to always love you."

She cups my face and peppers me with a bunch of kisses. "You think I loved you because I thought this would be easy? This life is anything but easy, but loving you, it's the easiest thing I've ever done. Boomer is wrong. I know I'm young, but I knew I loved you the moment I saw you, Jesse."

"You better go get Eric."

She straightens and nods. "You must be in so much pain and here I am, blabbering."

"I love your blabber and love you, but I want him to clean me up so I can fuck you how I want."

Her lips shape into an O. "Oh."

"Oh is right." My pain might be hitting the top of the scales, but my cock is raging. I need to be inside her, feel her heat, feel how wet she is, and how she says my name when she comes.

"You are in no shape for that," she says on a half moan when I run my hand down her chest and twist her hard nipple.

"Doll, I'm in any shape I want to be in. Go get him because once my back is patched up, you better believe I'm going to fuck you so hard you'll feel me for days."

She tilts her head back when I pluck her bud again. "I still feel you from earlier."

"You sore?" I cup her pussy through her dress, and that's when I notice she still hasn't changed, and I can feel my dried cum on her thighs.

"A little."

Her heat tickles my fingers, and part of me wonders if I want to fuck her right here and now in these blood-ridden sheets.

She pushes down on my hand, and that's when I remember I still have her panties. She's bare. She's ready.

"But I like it."

With a growl, the pain suddenly vanishes, and my body awakens. I fly off the bed, whisk her into my arms, and plant her against the wall. I spread her thighs and prepare to take what is mine.

CHAPTER TWENTY

Sarah

WE DIDN'T GET TO HAVE SEX FOR THE PAST THREE NIGHTS. Doc came down right as Jesse was about to fuck me against the wall.

I have a feeling that's going to be our thing.

He ordered Jesse to put me down and to lay in bed, and Jesse wasn't a happy man about that. His chest and shoulders heaved, and when he didn't listen, Doc did something I never thought he would do.

He sedated him.

Jesse has been asleep for three days so his wounds can heal. Apparently, Doc's professional opinion was if Reaper kept getting out of bed and ripping his stitches, it would take longer to heal, and the chance of infection would get worse. Jesse would have fought him on it too, so Doc did what he had to.

I've been by his side for three days, reading to him and

sleeping next to him. I don't know if he knows I'm here, but I like to think he does.

On the right of me is Moretti. There's been no change in his condition. Doc—I'm really trying my best to call people by their damn road name, but old habit dies hard—he believes that Moretti might have brain damage.

So I read to him too. I pull out a book, settle between the two men, and read science fiction novels. I hope they're imagining the stories and are in a dream state in another world.

I flip the page and am about to read the next chapter when the basement door opens and light spills through. That's another thing about this basement. There are no windows, so it's easy to lose track of time. When Tool comes into view, he doesn't look much better than Reaper, to be honest.

He still lives in guilt. My cheek is fine. A little sore and when I eat, my jaw clicks now, but no one needs to know that. "We can't find Boomer. Hawk's bike is gone. We don't know where he is, and his phone is off."

I set my cup of coffee down on the table and do my best not to lose my damn shit. I'm not sure what Boomer's problem is, but we need him here, especially now. Especially with Moretti's stepson wanting revenge on the MC, on me. It makes no sense. I have no enemies. I don't think I have them, anyway. I mean, bouncing around from foster home to foster home, I didn't have time to exactly make friends in order to turn them into enemies.

"Um, how does church work?" I ask, feeling a bit naïve that I'm talking to the head honcho here now that Jesse is unconscious. The VP takes over all responsibilities if something happens to the President, but the problem Tool has is that he doesn't know everything that is going on, and we need to be vigilant.

"Usually at the same time every day, but with him being down like this, I haven't called it. I've ordered everyone to stay at the clubhouse."

"Everyone?" I ask. "That's a lot of brothers."

"It's a hard time. People want to be here for Reaper, especially since we need to remain on high alert."

"Tool, I need to talk to you about something. Reaper didn't get a chance to tell you before Doc knocked him out."

That knowing smirk that all the men seem to have lifts the right side of Tool's beard as he grins. "Yeah, Doc is going to get an earful for that when he wakes up. It won't be pretty."

"No, it won't," I agree.

Tool drags a chair up and spins it around, and then swings his leg over the seat like it's a bike before sitting on it. "What do you need to talk about with me, Sarah?" He leans to the left a bit. "Your cheek looks better than it did. I'm still so sorry about that. It shouldn't have happened."

"Stop." I get up from my spot and make my way over to him, leaning against the bed that's closest. "It was an accident. Don't fret about it. It was my fault. I'm not even a little mad. I've moved on. You should too."

"I can't. Not without knowing if I'm going to lose my patch. The club is everything to me, Sarah. Everything. It's my home. It's my family."

"You aren't going to lose anything. I promise." I bend over and give him a hug. He doesn't hug me back for a few seconds, but when he does, he holds on tight like he has never been held before.

"I hope you're right," he mumbles into my neck. "Anyway..." Tool leans back into the chair and sighs. "What's so important that you want to call church?"

"I can't call it. You can." I point out.

"What's up? Are you going to tell me, or are we going to keep beating around the bush?"

"Reaper talked to Moretti before he got put in a coma."

"Shit, that guy must be in a lot of pain. He didn't seem bad. Him and Reaper seem to be on good terms. His guys are upstairs, and everyone is getting along well."

"Good. He said it was his stepson who did this. He was forced to tell Reaper to come to the hotel because his stepson was threatening his daughter. Before the hotel blew up, Moretti sent Reaper a text to stay away."

"Damn, that's fucked up."

"He also said that the stepson wants to break this MC; he wants to get to me."

"You?" Tool stood, sliding the chair back to its spot. He is alert, protective. "Why?"

"I don't know. I don't have enemies. I don't have friends. I keep to myself. I went to school, came here; anything before that was just foster homes."

"Shit, so the MC is a target, along with you?"

"It sounds like—" but I'm cut off by Reaper's sleep voice.

"It sounds like his stepson is going to kill whoever he has to that is a part of the club to get to Sarah."

I shake my head, and Tool makes a sound of disagreement. "But why blow up the hotel? Why try to kill Moretti?" Tool asks.

Reaper grunts and lifts his hand. "Water," he croaks. "Fuck, how long have I been out?"

"Three days." I hurry over to him and pour him a tall glass of cold water. "Here you go. Sip—"

He guzzles it down, and water spills from the corner of his lips.

"It," I finish saying, but not in time.

"More please, doll?"

"Anything for you, baby," I say, kissing him on the cheek before pouring another glass.

He drinks that glass down too, and then peeks under the sheet, cursing. "You have got to be fucking kidding me. I'm sick of these catheters in my dick. I want it out. Go get, Doc. I'm going to kill him."

"If you want to have sex again, you'll kill him after."

Reaper lifts his middle finger to Tool, and I giggle from the banter.

"Why does this kid want anything to do with us, Prez? Why the hell come after us?"

"He blew up the hotel because it is associated with us, and so is Moretti."

Reaper spoke about Moretti in the present tense, which only makes the air around us thicker because Moretti, while he is here, he isn't at the same time. He isn't breathing on his own, and the ventilator is doing it for him. Doc says it's to give his body a break to heal, but I'm not too sure that's really the reason.

"What do we do?" Tool asks. "We have no idea where he is, and it seems like the person who might know is in a coma. Can we wake him?"

"Not without causing him so much pain that it might send him into cardiac arrest."

"Shit." My hand flies to my heart. "You're going to cause me to have a heart attack if you sneak up like that on me again."

Doc laughs and jumps off the steps, ignoring the last four steps. "Sorry, Sarah. I wouldn't want that."

"What do we do if we can't wake him? Wait around until

he takes us out?" Tool questions all of us, but I know the question is really aimed at Reaper.

"Call for church. Tell everyone to be on alert. I want everyone carrying a gun at all times. Tell Boomer to get his crazy explosives and shit, and I want patrols around the clubhouse. Lock the gates. Install more cameras. It's time to lockdown."

"There's a problem with that, Prez."

"What?"

I fall in my seat and wring my hands together. "Boomer isn't here."

"Okay, so call him," Reaper says.

"No, Prez." Tool uncrosses his arms and swallows, nervous and a bit afraid that Reaper might punish him for what he is about to say. "Boomer is gone. He hasn't been back. Phone is off."

"He left?"

"Seems like it."

Reaper nods, sniffs, and clears his throat, obviously fighting emotion. "I see."

"He'll be back," I say. "He has to come back." Boomer said he'd never leave me. I thought we were closer than that. He and I grew inseparable. Apparently, I'm easier to leave than he said. What am I going to do without him? The MC won't be the same. Yes, I have Reaper, but if Boomer isn't here, my heart won't be complete.

Something will always be missing.

"I'll call church now. I'll let everyone know. I like seeing you awake. MC needs you."

"Tool?"

Tool turns his wide shoulders to the side to make it through the doorway and peeks over his round muscle.

"Don't think I've forgotten about the punishment I have in store for you for hitting Sarah. I haven't."

"Understood, Prez."

"You aren't losing your patch, so you can stop thinking that. You're my VP, and I know it was an accident. You're my best friend, but I can't let this go."

Tool's shoulders sag with relief, and he nods. "Thank you, Reaper. I'll take any punishment you give."

After Tool leaves, I crawl into the bed with Reaper, and Doc double checks his wounds. "You're looking good. You might just heal after all."

"Good. Now, get out. I want to be alone with my ol' lady."

I'll never get tired of hearing that. I cuddle into his side, and Doc turns down the lights, so they aren't as harsh.

"Let go, doll. It's okay. I got you." He kisses the side of my head and holds me tight as I do what he says, obeying him effortlessly.

I cry into the crook of his arm, the pain from Boomer leaving finally escaping. The sobs are grotesque, stomach turning. I feel like I'm going to be sick it hurts so much. He left. He said he'd never leave. I feel abandoned again. The one person I thought would always be here for me.

"Everyone always leaves me." I clutch his side, digging my fingers into his ribs as I hold onto him. Reaper has always been my anchor, the one man who saves me from destruction.

"Not everyone." He flips me over onto my back and pushes my hair out of my eyes. "I'm never going to leave you, doll. Never. I love you."

"I love you too."

"No, Sarah. Look at me. Open your eyes."

I had no idea I closed them.

"There you are." He brushes my tears away. "I love you so much that it is an obsession. It consumes me. It's unhealthy. I want to possess you. Every inch."

"You do. I'm yours, Jesse. Always have been."

He kisses me gently, taking my heart into his hands. "And always will be."

Always.

CHAPTER TWENTY-ONE

Reaper

I T'S BEEN AN ENTIRE WEEK, AND A FEW THINGS ARE REALLY STARTING to piss me off.

One, I haven't had sex since our first time.

Two, we haven't had sex.

And I'm fucking horny.

She's been parading around in these tiny little black lace panties, teasing me, provoking me, knowing damn good and well that I can't do anything about it because Doc threatened that if I did anything to open my wounds, he would put me in a medically-induced coma too.

But guess who has just been cleared?

"Still be careful!" Doc shouts at me, but all I can hear is my blood rushing through my veins, pure static blinding and drowning out any unnecessary noise. If it isn't Sarah crying out my name when my cock is planted deep, then everything is most definitely unnecessary.

Careful.

I'm done being careful. She's been teasing me for a week. How the hell can we have sex once, just once, and then she turns me down because of doctor's orders? It's fucking bullshit.

"Sarah!" My voice carries through the house.

"Oh, you're in trouble," Poodle taunts.

"Ye, shut it," Skirt says. "He won't like it that yer teasing his gal."

"He is right." I enter the main room without looking at anyone else and zero in on Sarah. She's playing pool with Tank, and the guy is sweating up a storm. I don't blame him. Anytime I get around her, I get hot and heavy too. "Sarah!"

"Stop bellowing; I'm here. Jeez." She lines up her shot and bends over, waving that ass in the air, fucking taunting me again. When I get her alone, I'm going to fucking spank her for the shit she has pulled the last week.

She hits the ball into the pocket and then grabs the chalk, never taking her eyes off me as she blows the excess off the tip. I can't wait to feel those lips around me. My time waiting to experience everything is over.

"Drop the stick and come with me."

"I will after this game," she says.

"You'll come now," I growl, deepening my voice so my authority is noticed. Tank gets the hint and drops the stick, putting his hands in the air in surrender.

The guy is way too skittish to be that big. It's such a contradiction.

"Is that so?" she says, ignoring me, and all the guys look everywhere else but us.

It's been a stressful time. I've been grumpy as fuck for a whole bunch of reasons. Badge found out who Moretti's stepson is, but he can't seem to locate him anywhere. The guy is in the wind, along with Boomer. Moretti is still in a coma, the only one who can give us answers, and my cock has been hurting for far too long.

I need to release all my pent-up frustration.

"Come here. Now, Sarah."

She licks her lips and places the stick on the table. She's wearing tight low-rise jeans and a purple shirt that's a little too short for my liking. Her flat stomach is showing, along with her golden skin that's meant for my eyes only. She saunters over to me, and I watch her movements. She glides, almost like a cat with how soft and elegant she floats across the floor to me. Damn it, never in my life has a woman commanded my attention like this.

"What is it, baby?" she asks and rubs her lips together. I inhale, smelling that goddamn cherry lip gloss that drives me up the wall.

I'm going to fuck that mouth with my cock and mess up that silky perfection that has messed with my mind for far too long. I say nothing else; I give her no warning. I throw her over my shoulder and slap her on the ass in front of everyone.

All the guys holler as I leave, celebrating my win. And it is most definitely a win.

She's a trophy I plan on admiring every fucking day for the rest of life.

I kick my door open and then slam it shut again. The room is still a little messy, but it's big, and the bed is freshly made. It's a bachelor pad, that's for sure. The curtains aren't even real curtains; they're a blanket. That will all change. Sarah has been dying to make changes to this place to make it feel like a home, and I'm going to let her do whatever she wants.

I toss her on the bed and watch her tits bounce under her shirt. "Get undressed," I growl, grabbing the back of my shirt collar to shuck it over my head.

Sarah gets on her hands and knees, crawling to me, that ass in the air again just begging for my hand. Once she gets to close enough to me, she flattens her tongue along my happy trail and licks all the way up until she gets to my lips, giving me a sloppy kiss. I hold her head still, making sure she can't move until I want her to.

And I want her to.

"Suck my cock, doll."

Her eyes dilate as she unbuttons my pants, and she trembles. "I've never—"

"I know, and I can't wait to fucking come down your throat knowing it's all mine."

"Jesse," she gasps.

"Don't call me that right now. Call me Reaper, understand?"

"Yes," she hisses as she wraps her hands around my dick, tugging down my jeans with her other. I don't know if my cock is really that big or if her hands are really that small; either way, she makes me feel like a king.

"Stop," I tell her, and she rises on her knees.

Her cheeks are rosy, and her lips are wet with that gloss still, but not for long. I fist the middle of her shirt, and with one quick yank, I rip it off her body. She's wearing a white satin bra, her tits spilling out of it, and her pink nipples are hard, fucking taunting me again.

I really love to be taunted.

"Take off your pants," I say, kicking mine off until I'm naked.

She stares at me, roaming her eyes over every inch of my

body. I'm all cut up still, burned, but I feel great. My tattoos are marred, and my body won't ever look the same, but she seems to like what she sees, and that's all that matters.

Her pants hit the wall, and the blonde tuft above her pussy gleams in the light. She didn't wear underwear today. Fuck.

"Spread your legs. Let me see you." I stroke my cock with both hands, squeezing tight like I know her pussy is. She does what I say, and her pink folds open for me when she pulls them apart with her fingers. Her clit is erect and swollen, and her sweet cream is leaking out of her cunt, inviting me in.

With a savage growl, I grab her legs and lift her hips off the bed until her pussy is a breath away from me. I don't wait any longer. I dive in, licking that cunt like I've been dreaming about. I hum in appreciation and lay my forehead above her belly to keep her still. She's wiggling, trying to get free as I feast.

I dive my tongue into her hole repeatedly, gathering that juice that I can't get enough of. It's better than any cigarette, drink, and drug that I've ever had.

"Reaper," she moans my name. "Fuck, Reaper. Oh, god. Yes. You're so good."

I fucking know.

She's better, though.

I lift her higher until only her head lies against the bed, and her hands are looking for something to hold on to; something better than the sheets. Moving my hands to her ass, I hold her globes tight, pushing her further into my face. I lick up, sucking her clit into my mouth and nibbling the candy.

It's enough to make her explode.

I push two fingers inside her heat, needing to feel her

muscle contract around me as she comes. I kiss her clit, appreciating it, adoring it, just like I would her lips. Every part of her body deserves the same amount of attention.

Her thighs shake, the muscle and skin jiggling from the spasms. She can't seem to stop. It's as if she is freezing, but I know better because there is a light coat of sweat all over her body that gives her body an eternal glow.

Gathering her juices, I slip out of her sheath and inch a little further back. I watch her face for any protest, but when all I see is lust, I decide to keep going. I push my wet fingers against her puckered star, swirling the tight muscle and lightly probing it; nothing too much, just enough to see where I stand.

"I want in here," I say.

"You won't fit, Reaper. You're too big."

"Not today, or tomorrow, but one day. We will work our way up to it." I slip my pinky inside, and she moans and pushes down, starting to ride my finger. "You are greedy for it, aren't you? You like all your holes filled. You're a little slut for me, Sarah. You gonna let me fuck all your holes?"

"Yes, they are yours." She squeezes her thighs as she thrust onto my hand.

"Damn right, they're mine. You're mine. You saved this body for me." I pull out and drop her legs onto the bed and crawl over her body, straddling her head. I grab the headboard and look down. "Suck me."

She stretches up and runs her tongue down the length before sloppily taking me between her lips. My body shudders from the first feel of her searing mouth around my cock. Leaning back, my eyes fall to her, watching her lashes flutter, and her lips stretch to accommodate me. When she places her soft amber irises on me, I nearly lose it.

I hold her head down and start to fuck her face, pumping my cock in and out as hard and deep as she will let me. Her nose hits my stomach, and my sack slaps against her chin. She can take me all the way down her throat.

"I'm going to come," I warn her. "Fuck! I'm going to come." Gritting my teeth, I pull my saliva-drenched cock free and lift her legs, thrusting into her in one fluid motion. She cries out, and on the third pump, I come just like I said I would, and fill her up. My hot seed is dripping from her, soaking my path to take her more.

I don't stop. I keep pounding, fucking her through my orgasm. I don't plan on leaving this bed all day and night. I want her pussy to cry from our lovemaking. Her golden-spun hair is fanned over the pillow, and every guttural groan that leaves her mouth is heaven.

It means I'm doing something right.

I slam into her as hard as I possibly can. I'm taking out every anger and stressor I had this week. It's an abusive pace. Some would call it punishing with how hard I'm fucking her, but guess what? My ol' lady fucking loves it. Her pussy is soaked, and she cries out for more.

"This cunt feels so tight, doll. You were made for me." I can't take my eyes off her round tits as they bounce from our movements. Her hands are above her head, and her mascara is smudged under her eyes. That cherry gloss is ruined, smeared all over her cheek and chin.

She's debauched and famished.

Just how I like her when we fuck.

I spread her legs as wide as they can, watching the show that my cock and her pussy are putting on for me. It's so riveting watching those pretty swollen folds suck me deep.

Strings of my cum are on my cock, coating me with every stroke.

She could be pregnant right now.

And the thought of my baby inside her, growing, tying her to me, it makes me fuck harder. I want that. I need it. "Fuck!" I scream when I lose all control. I pull out and flip her over, smacking her ass until a bright red mark is burning the pale cheek.

I press her head against the mattress with my hand and slide into her slowly. I brush my lips against her ear and groan from how good she feels. "I'm going to fill you up, doll. I'm going to have you leaking my cum for hours, for days. Every time you walk, you'll feel me there."

"I always feel you," she manages to say even though her lips are conflicted against the mattress.

I know what she means. I always feel her too. In my mind, my body, my soul, and in my damn bones. She's everywhere. Sarah has made my soul her house, and she is the one that anchors me home.

I kiss her cheek, neck, and lick down her spine. I stop fucking her. I need more. I want to see her. I flip us again and turn her around until she is straddling me now, staring at me through dazed eyes and red cheeks. The imprint of the sheets shows on the side of her face, and I grin, loving that I somehow leave these marks on her.

Her hands fall to my chest and skim over the scabs on my heart. "I'm so full in this position." She bites her lip when I thrust up, letting her get a feel of how good this is going to be.

"Ride me, doll. Show me how you want to fuck me."

She stays still, pressing her tits together from taking leverage on my chest with her hands. The pressure they bring, the small palms are nothing. I can barely feel the weight, but I'd know the touch anywhere. The way the warmth awakens me, only one woman does that, and she is right in front of me.

"I might be bad at it."

I cup her jaw with my hand and shake my head. "That's impossible. Everything with you feels better than anything I've ever experienced. It's you and me. It doesn't get better than that. Ride me, Sarah." My hands fall to her flared out hips, settling in that curve.

Made just for me.

I slide them up her lithe body, cupping her tits in my palm. There is a suntan line from her bikini. Her chest is tan, and her breasts are pale. The triangle shape of the bikini covers each mound, and the skinny straps tie up and around her neck.

Mmm, I can't wait to take her swimming because I know what is underneath that swimsuit.

I roll her nipples between my fingers, and she takes the first rock. It's slow and trepidatious, getting a feel for me being so deep inside her. Sarah rocks faster and cries out when I brush that spot inside her. She stops, staring at me with wide, surprised eyes and then, she does something I don't expect—she fucks me.

Really grinds her pussy against my cock.

My hands fall to the crook of her hips again, holding tight. I never take my eyes off her. I want to soak up every expression she makes. Her pussy is getting wetter. Our skin slaps together, my sack pulling tight to my body, warning me about my next orgasm.

"Oh god, Reaper." She squeezes my pecs and rocks faster. The bed slams against the wall, and this time I'm the one shouting, holding back my cum as long as I can until I feel her clench around me.

"Come with me!" I shout. "Sarah!" I can't hold back anymore. She's too good. "Damn it! Oh, fuckkk! Take it, doll. Take it." I press her hips against me harder, continue to violently rock, and sneer to keep myself from blacking out. The edges of my eyes blur, but I have to see her fall apart.

Just like I am.

"Reaper!" she screams, leaning back as the first wrack of her body vibrates my cock. She throws her head back, the sweaty ends of her hair tickle my thighs, and her hands grip my legs. Every spasm of her pussy buckles her body, and another spurt of cum leaves me as she milks me.

She falls forward, laying her cheek on my chest. We don't move; we don't dare to. We lay in silence, trying to catch our racing breaths as the thunder rolls outside, threatening a storm. It won't compare to the hurricane that just happened in here.

Sarah is a force to be reckoned with.

My cock is still inside, and she kisses my chest, the spot that almost killed me. It reminds me of Bullseye when he throws his darts.

"Next time, I want you to wear my cut." Just the thought has my cock twitching in her cunt.

"Oh?" She reaches for it and slips it on, the lapels covering her tits. "How about right now?"

Fuck yeah, I'm one lucky son-of-a-bitch.

CHAPTER TWENTY-TWO

Sarah

"**S**ARAH, YOU GOT A PACKAGE!" POODLE SLAMS THE METAL door and shakes it. "It's light." Next, he presses his ear to it. "Silent. What did you order? Is it panties?"

Skirt scuffs Poodle on the back of the head. "Don't ask Reaper's ol' lady about her panties!"

"I was just wondering!"

"Don't wonder about her panties, Poodle!" Reaper shouts from the basement.

Poodle's jaw drops. "How did he hear that?"

"It's his ol' lady. He has bionic hearing when it comes to her," Pirate slurs, taking another swig of rum. I worry about him. He always has a bottle of rum in his hand. There isn't a day when he isn't drinking. What's his story? What happened to him to make him want to drink his life away?

I snag the box from Poodle's hands and tuck it under my

arm. "Whatever you think it is, pretend it is because I'm never telling you a thing."

"Mean. Just mean." Poodle drops his head as he walks toward the bar like his favorite toy got taken away.

"Stop wondering about her panties, Poodle!" Reaper yells from the basement again.

Poodle scoffs, spreading his arm out to point at the basement door. "How?"

I giggle and sit on the black leather loveseat. Hmm, I don't remember ordering anything. Maybe it's from Reaper, and maybe it is panties or something dirty. With that thought, I tear the tape off and rip it right down the middle, excited to see the gift he got me, us. I grab ahold of the rough cardboard edges and spread the top open to see paper. I push it aside and freeze when the paper starts to turn red.

Wet.

Dripping.

I swallow, trying to find the courage to open it. I'm afraid to see what it is. I lift my head from the box and look around to make sure no one is paying attention to me. My palms sweat, and my heart pounds against my chest, like a wrecking ball slamming against a solid, strong structure ready to break me down. Carefully, I pinch the paper that doesn't have blood on it and move it to the side.

Loud pants raise my chest when I see a letter that says, "I have something you love." It's in a plastic bag, the paper clean and white, stark against the blood. I nudge the plastic bag out of the way and scream.

I can't breathe. Oh god, I can't breathe. I can't think. I shove the box off my lap, and everything slows. My vision blurs, my chest tightens, my lungs—I can't feel my lungs working. The taste of my own blood coats my throat, and hot tears sting my cheeks. I fall off the couch and onto the floor. The wood rubs my knees raw from the force of the fall, and Skirt catches me around my waist, so I don't fall face-first onto the ground.

A few other brothers come and help me onto the couch. Reaper's roar can be heard from the basement as he climbs the steps to get to me. His boots shake the entire clubhouse as he tries to get to me as fast as he can. He pushes all the guys out of the way and picks me up, lifting me onto his lap.

"Sarah, what is it; what's wrong?"

But I still can't think; I can't figure out how to breathe. I point a shaky finger to the box, and Tool bends down to grab it. A few lumps of paper fall on to the floor, blood dripping off the corner of the box. Tool gives Reaper a quick glance and takes the Ziploc bag out where the letter is safe.

"Holy shit," he whooshes as one breath.

"What?" Reaper growls. "Give it to me."

"No! Keep it away from me. It's Boomer! It's Boomer," I sob. I do my best to wiggle my way out of Reaper's hold, but he squeezes me tight. I'm trapped. I can't run. I have nowhere to go.

"Okay, okay. Tool has it. You're okay. What is it? I need to know."

Bile inches its way up my throat when I think of the bloody finger in the box. "It's Boomer's finger."

"What?" Reaper sounds devastated and almost like he doesn't believe me.

"I'd know that finger anywhere. It's the one that has the deep cut on it from the hook. The one time when you guys went fishing. He told me that story. It's his favorite memory of you." I remember sitting on my bed, watching TV alone when

REAPER

Boomer came into my bedroom. I was sixteen and had been with the MC for a few weeks. I was still scared. I didn't trust anyone—not even Boomer. I had learned he was my brother, but that meant nothing. I learned long ago that trust is something so easily broken, so easily shattered, that the person does not matter. Boomer worked long and hard to get to know me, and when he handed me a can of pepper spray, I saw the gnarly looking scar. It was ugly and jagged, the scar huge and puffy because the only thing they had to stitch it together was another hook and fishing line.

Reaper sets me down and kisses my forehead. I wrap my arms around my legs and place my chin on my knees, thinking about Boomer and where he could be. All this time, I thought he had left, but what if he has been tortured? Reaper picks up the box, and a trembling breath leaves him when he sees the finger.

"There's a message for you, Reaper."

I turn in the loveseat and see Tool on the ground, putting the paper together like it's a puzzle.

Him for her.

"That's it?" Reaper roars. "No! No. Absolutely not. I'm calling church. Meet me in the chapel, now!" he screams, kicking the box across the room. He bends over and takes my chin in his hands, giving me a hard kiss. "I'm not going to let anything happen to you. I'm going to get him back. I promise."

Whoever has Boomer wants me.

And I'm going to give them what they want.

I haven't told anyone, but there is another sheet of paper in my hand that I'm hiding from anyone. It's an address.

And I plan on going.

I give Reaper a nod, and a stampede of boots hurry to the

chapel. I'm alone. The note for Reaper stares at me, mocking me. I wait a few minutes to make sure I'm alone, and when I know that I'm good, I punch the address into my phone and crumble the paper up then throw it on the ground.

If I walk out this door, there's a chance I won't be coming back. It's a chance I have to take. Boomer would do this for me. I have to do it for him. I leave my heart behind. Glancing over my shoulder, I stare at the door that Reaper is behind. My life has been so good, and at least I got a taste of what it was like to be with him, even if it was only for a little bit.

I can die a happy woman knowing what it is like to have Reaper's love.

I open the front door as quietly as I can, take one last look at the home that's been mine for the last two years, and close the door behind me. When I turn around, I run smack into a chest, and a piece of cloth is shoved over my mouth.

"Good girl," the stranger says, just as my eyes roll back and the unknown takes me.

"Sarah."

My name is whispered, and it echoes all around me.

"Come on. Wake up, Sarah!"

Chains rattle, and my head throbs. I wince when I move my neck and groan.

"That's it. Wake up, sis. Come on. I really need you to wake up."

Boomer. That's Boomer's voice. Opening my weighted lids, everything is fuzzy. It takes a minute for things to come into focus, and when it does, it's something from a horror movie. It's dark, really dark, with red lights every few feet. I'm in a warehouse of some sort, old, rusted barrels sit on the ground around me, and large chains hang from the ceiling.

"Sarah."

I whip my head to the right and see Boomer. His hands are chained over his head, toes barely dragging against the floor, and dried blood rivers down his arm from the man cutting off his finger. "Boomer!" I cry, tugging on the iron bracelets around my wrists. They're tight, rubbing me raw. My skin tears and breaks, but my wrists do not come free. "Oh my god, Boomer. Are you okay?" I try to keep myself together. I try not to cry. I need to be strong right now.

He looks beaten and whipped. Welts are all over his body, and one eye is swollen shut. The chain rattles above him as he tugs on them weakly, staring at me with one good eye. "Are you okay? Did he hurt you?"

"No, I'm fine. I feel fine. My head kind of hurts, but that's it. What are you doing here? I thought you left." I keep it out of my voice that I thought he left me.

"I did," he says, hurting me further. "I planned on coming back, but I got jumped from behind and brought here. He wanted information on you, but I wouldn't give you up. I'd never give you up. I was ready to die, but he got you here somehow."

"I got your finger priority fucking mail. Of course, I'm here."

"Hey, did you put it on ice? Might be able to sew it back on."

"That's what you're thinking about right now? We need to get out of here!" I hiss, tugging on the damn iron again.

"I've been hanging here for a few days. I've had a lot of time to think, so yeah, I was curious about my finger."

"What does he want?" I jerk away when I hear the teeth clattering and light chirps of rats scurrying along the floor.

"I'm not sure, but I know he is fascinated with you. I think after Moretti got into business with Reaper, the guy has been counting the days until he could get you alone. I think you know him, Sarah. You have to."

"It's impossible. I don't know a soul besides David." My heart squeezes in my chest. "It's not David is it?"

"David wouldn't be able to get the upper hand on me." Boomer sounds offended by the accusation, but I'm not trying to have a pissing contest. "I don't know who it is."

A door opens in the distance and echoes when it shuts, a loud bang sounding reminding me of a sawed-off shotgun. Footsteps get closer, and I can hear mumbling as well. Someone is talking to themselves. It's too dark to tell where the person is, but when the red light in front of me becomes shadowed, and boots touch my bare feet, it doesn't take long to figure out the person in question is right in front of me.

"Long time no see, Sarah." His voice his hoarse, sounding injured and broken. "Last time I saw you, you were little. My, my, you've grown up pretty."

"Stay away from her, you sick fuck! I'll kill you if you touch her. I'll fucking kill you!"

"Shut up!" The man backhands Boomer, and the sound of something breaking snaps.

"No! Leave him alone. What do you want? I'll give you whatever you want, okay? Just let him go."

"I'm not letting either of you go. You have no idea how much you have ruined my life!"

"I don't know you," I whimper. "Please, we have money. We will give you whatever you want."

"I want you to watch me torture him. He is your brother, right?"

"Please, don't hurt him," I sob, watching Boomer spit out a wad of blood.

"I wanted to be your brother, and you left me." The cock of a gun grinds the barrel. The red glow shines between the chains around Boomer's arms, and the man holds it against Boomer's shoulder.

"Do it," Boomer seethes. "Shoot me. It doesn't matter. I'll fucking kill you one way or another."

"Not if I kill you first." A loud gunshot rings through the air.

"No!" I scream. "No."

I have a feeling my world just came to an end.

CHAPTER TWENTY-THREE

Reaper

"**W**AKE HIM UP!" I YELL AT THE TOP OF MY LUNGS. Tool and Tongue are holding me back from murdering Doc. He won't listen to me. "I swear to god, if you don't do as I say, you won't be able to walk for the rest of your life."

"I can't wake him, not yet."

"Sarah's life is in jeopardy! You're not going to do this for her? You saved her all those years ago! Wake him up!" I strain against the arms holding me back, grunting and giving it everything I have to get free so I can kill him.

"Sarah is important to all of us, but if I wake him, there is a good chance he will die. His body isn't healed—"

"I don't give a fuck. If he is a casualty, then so be it. I don't give a fuck." Hot tears spring to my eyes when I think about Sarah being in danger. Who knows where she is at? All I know is when I walked out of the chapel, to see

an empty main room and the front door wide open, I lost
my fucking mind.

Her necklace was on the steps, the clasp broken, and the
diamond shining as beautiful as Sarah's smile does. It took five
men to restrain me, to stop me from getting on someone's bike
and going after her.

Only I have no idea where she is.

Someone took her, though, and I know it has to do with the
package she got in the mail.

Moretti's goons point guns at us, and my men do the same.
We stare each other down, barrels against barrels, the promise
of death lingering in the air, and one of the goons has the nerve
to cock his gun.

"No one is getting near him," he says in a thick Italian
accent.

"I will kill all of you if you don't wake him up. Doc, Eric," I
say his name. I never say their names, but I'm desperate. "Please."

"One minute," he says, holding up his index finger. "One
minute, and that's all you get, or his heart will fail. Do you understand that?"

"One is all I need." I finally calm and rip my arms free of
Tool and Tongue. "I'm fine." Tool goes to grab for me again, but
I shove him away. "I said I was fine." I'm not fine. I'm fucking
losing it. "Tool, I want you to go search that box again, find any
clues. There had to have been one, something other than that
damn note."

"You got it, Prez."

"Take me downstairs. Wake him."

Eric is about to argue with me. I can tell. He opens his
mouth and closes it again, snapping his jaw shut. "Alright, but
if he dies—"

"He won't die." One of the goons nudges the gun against Eric's head. "Or you die."

"Ye better think real long and hard on that, mate," Skirt says a bit too happily, holding two guns in his hands as he points them at two different people. There are only four of them, and the other two are downstairs.

The man, Michael, isn't too happy. He curves his lip and holsters his weapon, giving in to my demand. Eric shakes his head the entire way down the steps as I follow him. I really don't care if he agrees with it or not. I need answers. Moretti has them.

It's as simple as that.

"He might not wake up right away. It may take hours." Doc opens the drawers next to the bed and pulls out a syringe, clear with medicine.

"I don't have hours." I knock a pitcher over, and water flies everywhere. It doesn't faze Doc. "She could be dying right now!"

"I can't control how long it takes for the medicine to work! You want shit done now, I understand, but I can only do so much! Be patient." Doc inserts the needle in the IV, and I wait for any sign of life.

Nothing happens.

One minute.

Five minutes.

Fifteen minutes.

Nothing.

"Wake the fuck up, Moretti!" I wrap my hand around his throat, and one of his men puts a gun to my head.

"Hands off."

I elbow him in the nose, the crunch of bone shattering against my arm. I smile, satisfied. "How about you fuck off?"

REAPER

"Reaper," Doc says my name to get my attention, and when I look down, Moretti's eyes are darting back and forth behind his lids. "One minute, remember." Doc turns off the ventilator, and when Moretti feels him pull the tube out, his heart starts to race, and he panics, screaming from the pain. Doc gives him morphine and he calms a bit, but screams are still screams, no matter the pain level.

"Listen to me. Sarah and Boomer have been taken. She is my ol' lady, and Boomer is my kid. Your stepson sent us his fucking finger. I need to know where he could have taken them and why he wants Sarah. I won't let you go back under without telling me."

He stares at me through an eye that has no eyelashes; they were burned off in the explosion. I bend down when he opens his mouth, his voice harsh, the sound of sandpaper. "Don't know why," he gasps. "Try warehouses. He loves warehouses. He moves drugs. Lots of drugs. I'm sorry…" His voice cuts off when another seizure takes him, and Doc pushes all of us out of the way, pissed off that he ended up being right.

I might have killed the man.

In a record amount of time, Doc has Moretti in a medically induced coma again. Sweat drips from his brow, and his hands shake. He shoves by me, throwing his shoulder against mine. I hate that I had to do it, but it's more information than I had before. Moretti said warehouses and that he runs drugs. I know one other gang that moves drugs like that, and those are the Vegas Vipers. Maybe they will have some answers.

"Reaper!" Badge hurries down the steps. "I have something. I know how they're connected. Come on."

I take three steps at a time, and when I get to the kitchen, all the brothers are there. Tongue is sitting at the table, sharpening his blade, his dead eyes glaring at the space in front of him where Sarah used to sit. She would help him sharpen all his blades; she was the only one who cared about his weird fascination, and now I couldn't imagine not having him. If there is one thing I want Tongue to do, I want to make sure Moretti's stepson never speaks again.

Seeing all the support is emotional. I want to get on the road, though, and get to the Vipers. I don't care who I have to kill, what I have to do, and how many bullets are used. I'll find Sarah, and all who get in my way will be left as rotting corpses.

"Talk to me."

Badge taps away on his computer, looking more like one of us than a cop these days. He has a long beard, short-clipped hair that is still military style, but the hard look in his eyes, I've seen that before. It's a look a man gets when he doesn't care much about the law anymore.

"Sarah grew up in foster care, right?" he asks.

"Yeah, why?" I cross my arms and lean against the washer and dryer.

"Well, she bounced around a lot before she came here. Fifteen homes, to be exact. All of them sucked. They were the kind of parents who were only in it for the check. They had up to eight kids, most with records. When she finally landed at that last place, there was one kid who didn't take it so well."

"What's that mean? Moretti's stepson was never in foster care. That would make no sense."

"It would if the woman he married had a drug problem and lost custody of him for fifteen years. She got her head on straight when she met Moretti, but the drugs ended up taking her in the end. Anyway, while the kid, Fabian Trullo, was in foster care, anytime Sarah got placed in a new home, he got placed there too. Out of fifteen homes, he was in thirteen of them with her. They basically grew up together. In some sick way, I think this guy looks at her as his sister. That's why he has Boomer. That's why he wants Sarah. In his head, it's always been him and her."

"Then why hasn't she ever said anything about him?" I wonder. The lingering doubt in the back of my mind makes me think that maybe this guy was her first love. It's a sick thought, but I know horrible things happen in foster homes; what if he did them to her? What if she is so used to his manipulation, she does exactly what he says.

"She has no idea this guy thinks of her that way. Most likely, this guy watched her from afar, became obsessed with her, stalked her, and got to know everything about her without her knowing a damn thing about him."

"So he wants vengeance."

"He wants Sarah. I've seen this before, unfortunately. It's your typical, 'If he can't have her, no one can' situation. He will kill anyone who gets in his way."

"Does Moretti know about this?" Because if he did, the man is dead, right now.

"Most likely not. By the time his stepson came back home, he was practically grown, a stranger, and had the mindset of a sociopath. The hate had been there for years, building and building for Moretti. He had been plotting for years, and when he found out Moretti got into business with you"— Badge snaps his fingers—"that's what pulled that mental trigger. It seemed no matter what, everyone got Sarah except him. He learned about Boomer, about you; probably still watched her in the distance, and you guys had no idea."

"Why now?" I ask. "Why wait until now? He had two years—"

"Why not? She's eighteen now." He swallows, clearly uncomfortable with what he is about to say. "He waited."

"He waited..." I say dumbly. "Waited for what?"

"The same thing you waited for, Prez. You waited until you could legally claim her." Tongue licks his knife, eyes rolling back when he feels the cold steel. "He doesn't look at her as his sister; it's more than that. She's his focus in life. He has a twisted delusion of her." He slides his eyes to me. "He wants her for himself."

"Tongue is right," Badge says. "Cases like this, it goes deeper than the bond between brother and sister, and that's only one-sided. He is dependent on her. He probably thinks since she can think for herself, she'll choose to be with him. He wants to be her father, brother, friend, lover; he wants to be all of it."

I've seen a lot of fucked up shit in my life but hearing this makes me want to be sick. The thought of her; no, no—I can't think like that.

Poodle pats my shoulder along with a few others, and I scrub my hands over my face, my tired eyes heavy from stress. "How many warehouses do the Vipers own?" I ask. I have a feeling I can find Moretti's son there.

"Five," he says.

"You can narrow that down to the ones that are most isolated," Badge says. "He wants to keep them away from people."

There's another meaning behind those words. Fabian took them somewhere that no one can hear their screams. Isolation. "Wait," an idea is brewing. "What's the most isolated thing in Vegas?"

"The desert," Badge says with a grin. "Fucking genius, Reaper." The confidence fades along with the smile. "Never mind. No warehouses in the desert that the Vipers own. I can't find it."

I snarl, slamming my fist down on the counter. "It's there. I can guarantee you it isn't in your system. Boys, wheels up. We have Vipers to see."

I plan to cut the head of every last one of them.

CHAPTER TWENTY-FOUR

Reaper

A HERD OF BIKES ROAR DOWN LONELIEST ROAD. DESERT IS ON either side of us, no building in sight. The Vipers clubhouse is a few miles past the strip on the other side, a place we usually stay far away from because of what Moretti did to their president.

Well, that truce is over.

I'm going to dismantle that club one by one and make sure those damn snakes can't poison me again. A piece of shit, run-down building comes into view on the side of the road. It looks like an old bar, something passersby usually stop at for a quick beer since it's the only thing for miles until someone wants to drive all the way back to the strip. Twenty of us pull to a stop in front of the wooden piece of shit. I wish Boomer was here because he'd blow this shit to the ground.

Fuck, I miss him.

"Bullseye, Tool," I call for my main two men. "Decide who

stays and who comes with us inside. I want people out here just in case anyone unexpected pulls up."

"You got it," Tool says the same thing he always does.

"I want a minute alone in there." I rub the handle of my gun under my vest, and Bullseye follows my hand. He nods, trusting me to take care of it.

"One minute and then I'm coming in," he says.

Seems to be the new time limit these days.

The porch creaks under my weight. I don't bother knocking. I lift my leg and kick the door down, the rotten wood giving without a problem. Cut-sluts huddle in the corner and cry, screaming when they see me. A few of the Vipers are caught off guard, and one tries for his gun, only I'm quicker. I cock my gun and shoot him right between the eyes, just like something out of an old west movie.

"Everyone better sit down and shut the fuck up, or you will all die. You're outnumbered and outgunned." I walk through the establishment. Whoever is in charge of this place should be ashamed of themselves. Flies swirl everywhere, and lines of uncut coke are on the table with stacks of cash. Hmm, I don't like that shit in my city.

The Vipers sit and put their hands in the air. Some are passed out from the drugs, and some even look dead. "I want to know who works with Fabian Trullo, Moretti's stepson." I place the warm barrel on the temple of the man who has the patch that says VP. That's a damn joke. "I have a feeling you know."

"Nope," he says.

I laugh as Tongue walks through what used to be the door. Ah, just the man I want to see. "Tongue? This guy isn't telling me what I need to know."

"Is that right?" he drawls, taking out his new shiny knife.

The man stares at the long, curved blade with big eyes, and Tongue twists the steel in the air. "Pretty, isn't she? I worked long and hard on her. Made her myself. She cuts through skin so softly. It's beautiful. She's the perfect work of art." Tongue grips the man by the back of the head and then shoves his hand into the man's mouth, pinching his tongue and pulling it out. "You might want to tell my President where Fabian is, or you won't be able to ever lick pussy again."

The man whimpers and nods in quick beats. I give him a chance and give Tongue a silent nod to let him go. He does, but he shoves the steel into the man's thigh, causing him to scream. A few Vipers try to get up and run, but my men stop them, guns pointed to their heads. The Vipers are way too high to try to defend themselves. They sit and shut up while their VP clutches his leg, whimpering like a little bitch.

Has the man never experienced pain before?

"Sorry, I wanted to see how she'd do penetrating bone." Tongue jerks the knife free, the blade still in perfect condition. No chips or dents from the bone. "Oh, yeah. She's a fucking gem. Just think about what she will do to your tongue." He shivers, a delightful smile on his face. I look down and notice his cock is getting hard.

Holy shit, the man gets off on this.

"If it isn't your tongue I take, it will be someone else's," he looks around the room, deciding on which man will be his victim.

"Speak," I tell him. "Where is Fabian? He has my ol' lady. And you know how us bikers are about our women."

He has a look of pure terror on his face, and he takes a few deep breaths to try to push through the pain of the wound in his leg. "Okay, okay," he says. "Fabian came to us; said he'd pay for one of our off-the-grid warehouses. He gave us a bunch of drugs to call it even. I had no idea he was going to take your ol' lady. I swear to god, man. If I had known he had anything to do with the Ruthless Kings, I would have never gotten into business with him."

"Where. Is. He?" I do everything I can to not blow this fucker's head off right here and now. Sarah hasn't been gone a day, and I'm losing my fucking mind. How will I live with myself if I don't get there in time?

What if I don't get there in time to save Boomer too? Hell, Boomer could already be dead.

No, I can't accept that. Boomer is smart. He knows how to live. I taught him well. He'll be fine. I know for a fact that if it came down to it, he'd save Sarah's life by sacrificing his own. It shouldn't bring me comfort, but it does.

"It's underground. You won't be able to see it from the road."

"Where? I won't ask again." I shove my gun into his mouth.

He mumbles around it, so I rip the warm barrel from his lips. "It's five miles north and three miles west in the middle of the desert. You'll see a shack, something rundown and broken. On the inside on the ground is a big metal door. I swear to god, that's where they are. That's the place he wanted." The man starts to cry, for good reason too.

No way am I going to leave him alive when he could retaliate. "Okay, thanks, boys. Fellas, have your way." I tuck my gun in my vest and walk out, the wood from the porch crunching under my boot. Gunshots and screams ring behind me, but I don't look back.

A man never looks back.

All that's left is to blow it up, and I'll save that for Boomer when we get him back. I swing my leg over the bike I'm borrowing from Tool; he had a few in the garage for backup. I wait outside for my men, and Skirt rolls his bike next to me, looking at the open door and hearing the pleas of people begging for their life.

"Did ye get what you needed?" he asks, his red beard shining like fire on his face as the sun bears down on us.

"I did." A few minutes later, the screams die down, and Vipers' cut-sluts run out the door, blood on their bodies. There are a few cars out here, and they each get into one, spinning out of the parking lot and zipping down the road to put this place in their rearview.

Tongue walks out and throws someone's pink appendage across the porch, and then he wipes his hands on his jeans. He inhales the summer air and smiles like he hasn't smelled the outdoors in days; he seems so happy. He has a pep in his step as he practically prances to his bike.

"Alright, boys. Five miles north and then three miles west inland. Let's ride," I shout, and at the same time, all of us crank our bikes, the engines rumbling like thunder. I don't mind the speed limit. I go as fast as I can without risking my life, eating up the five miles quickly. The road is long and flat with a few small hills. The air is hot, over a hundred degrees, and my skin sweats underneath the leather cut.

I'm thirsty for vengeance.

At five miles, I come to a stop. I hold out my left arm and take an immediate turn, cutting through the desert. There's a soft trail from other bikes that I see, so I follow it. Dust flies in all directions, and the rocks make the ride bumpy. I do my best to miss the dead plants and cactuses, but I know regardless the bikes are going to need worked on after this.

Three miles later, I see the shack the VP talked about. I still don't feel guilty for killing him. He was a means to an end. I don't even wait to come to a stop. I jump off my bike and let it fall to the ground then run inside the damn hut. There, right there is the metal door. I wrap my hands around the handles and pull, but there's no give.

"Fuck! Come on!" I give it all I have, planting my feet and tugging. The hinges groan and protest, the lock fights me back, but nothing will stop me from getting to her. Not when I know she is right beneath my feet. I've kept her safe for two years, and I won't let it come to an end now.

Tool grabs the handles too, and I spare him a grateful glance as both of us pull. The door snaps open, hinges fly and smack the walls of the shack. The door on the right hangs down, dangling. I kick it in and jump down, not thinking how far or unsafe it is.

I have one thing on my mind. Well two, but the first is Sarah and then Boomer. I'm not sure when he became secondary, maybe the moment she came into our lives. I get my gun out, and a few of my men drop down behind me. Fuck, it smells down here. Fabian must live in this dump.

It's dark and hot. If it's a hundred degrees outside, then it is one-hundred and thirty down here. Sweat is running down my face in lakes, stinging my eyes, burning them, and it hinders my vision. I wipe it away, gun held out in front of me, and Tool takes out a flashlight and points.

"Fuck. Me." He whistles, swiveling the light around. Chains hang from the ceiling and hooks, barrels of I don't know what sit everywhere, and they have biohazard symbol on them. Tool takes his screwdriver and pries open the top and picks up a pound of cocaine. There must be hundreds of barrels full of this stuff down here.

Tongue cuts the package open with the same knife he used to kill someone with and sprinkles a bit of the white powder in his mouth. He shakes his head, coughs, and then gags, "Shit, that's uncut. That's fucking sick. Millions of dollars' worth, at least." I'm not going to ask how he knows that. All of us have pasts.

I hear a clank of metal in front of us, and Tool shines his light down the darkened path, another door up ahead.

I can't wait any longer. I sprint to the door and just as I'm about to kick it in. Tool pulls me back by my shoulder. "We need to be quiet. We don't know what he is doing. We don't want to kill anyone he may have in his hands."

Tool reaches for the handle and turns it. What I see sends me in a downward spiral.

CHAPTER TWENTY-FIVE

Sarah

BOOMER IS JUST HANGING THERE. I DON'T KNOW IF HE IS DEAD or alive, but the blood, oh god, the smell of it is making me sick.

"You don't know how long I've waited for this, Sarah." The stranger runs his knuckles down my face and then brings his rancid mouth to my cheek. He smells disgusting, like body odor and smoke. It almost makes me gag.

"Who are you? Just tell me." I give in, wanting to know if I can salvage this situation any by talking to him.

"I can't believe you don't remember me. That's okay. We have the rest of our lives to get to know each other. I know you. We were in the same foster homes for a long time. Do you remember the Pines' house? The boy who broke his arm from falling off the roof?"

Of course, I remember that. It was terrible but being in

those houses was like another life to me. I barely remember anything, but the boy who fell, he nearly died. That much I remember. The next day, I couldn't ask how he was because I went to another home.

"That was me. You were the first person to run out and check on me. And from there, I knew we were meant to be together, but everyone else kept getting in my way. Everyone. First, it was that horrible man who almost killed you. I would have saved you from that. I would have. You need to believe me. Do you?" He is right in front of my face now, and when the red-light shines on him, I push against the barrel.

He reminds me of the devil with the red light on him. Sunken cheeks, black eyes, patchy red skin; he is a junky. "I believe you," I whisper.

"And then Boomer happened, and that damn MC. Do you know how hard it was to watch you with them around? To make sure you were safe. We have been together most of our lives, Sarah. My father is a very powerful man; we can go anywhere. We can sin, we can live, we can love." He presses his lips against mine, and I yank my head away, this time, throwing up all over the floor with how bad his breath is.

"I don't love you. The man I love will find me, and when he does, he will kill you."

"My name is Fabian," he says, ignoring the threat I just gave. It might be useless, but it makes me feel like there is some sort of hope. Thinking about Reaper is the only thing keeping me level and calm, and as long as I am alive, I have faith that he will find me and bring me home.

I don't know a man named Fabian. I don't remember a boy I always knew. Half of my childhood has no memory. I keep it blocked out. "Fabian?" I pretend to be amazed. "Oh my god, that's you? I didn't recognize you. You scared me with all of this. You could have just talked to me. Hurting Boomer wasn't necessary."

"You only have room for one brother in your life," he says, giving Boomer a jealous stare. "I hate him. I have always hated him. He isn't good for you like I am."

"I know, but I had no idea where you were." I shrug. "I had to make the best out of a bad situation, you know?" Every word slices like the thick lashes betrayal leaves behind.

"I know," he says. "But you have me now."

"I do. It's been so long. We have so much catching up to do. Unlock my wrists. Let's get out of here. You and me," I say.

"I-I don't know." He scratches his head. "What if you turn your back on me."

"Why would I do that?" I ask at the same time as I study my surroundings. "Come on, all these years and you don't trust me? Wow, that hurts, Fabian."

"I never want to hurt you." He takes my aching wrists in his hands and caresses the top of my hand.

God, if I make it out of here alive, I'm going to soak in a tub full of acid to get this man's touch off me. The guys at the MC have a few loose screws, like Tongue, but this guy is off his fucking rocker.

"Okay, but we have to leave right away, alright?" he says.

"Anything you want, Fabian." I make his name sound like a moan, a purr, a desperate need that needs to be filled inside me, and his eyes lock with mine, void of any emotion except insanity.

He hurries, sliding the key in the bracelet locks, and with one click, I'm free. I rub my wrists to get feeling back into them and give him a thankful smile. "Just a second. I can't feel my hands."

"No time to waste." He grips my arm and lifts me up. Fabian drags me forward, and I'm barely able to keep my feet under me. I run into chains and buckets, nearly tripping. Puddles splash beneath my feet, and I cringe, wondering what the liquid could be.

Boomer is up ahead, and right next to him is a double hook. On purpose, I hit my brother to see if there are any signs of life, and when I hear a quiet groan, I breathe a little easier. There is hope.

Fabian is in front of me, humming a tune I don't know, and I kick a metal pipe on the ground.

A loose metal pipe. I reach down and pat the floor as fast as I can, and Fabian turns around, staring down at me.

His hope turns wicked.

"What the fuck are you doing?"

I wrap my fingers around the bar and grin. "Getting out of here alive." I slash the pipe through the air and hammer his chest, a battle cry leaving my mouth when I swing to the other side and bash the pipe on the other side of his face. The chain from the ceiling gives when I tug on it, and the double hooks lower. I take Fabian by the shirt and slam his body against it, and then I click the power box that tightens the chain and lifts whatever is on the hook up.

Fabian's screams don't even bring solitude. I won't have any until I know he is dead. The hooks get deeper, penetrating through each of his shoulders until he is hanging there, stuck in mid-air.

"Sarah!" Reaper's voice is a whisper in the loud cries of Fabian. "Sarah!"

"I'm here!" I drop the pipe and turn around. Reaper is running right at me, gun lifted and the bullet breezes by me, landing right in the chest of the outlier known as Fabian.

Reaper cradles me into his chest, mimicking how someone holds a baby, and kisses my forehead. "God, I thought I lost you. Never do that to me again."

"I had it under control," I say, watching the men lower Boomer to the ground. "Is he okay? Please, let him be okay. He took so much abuse, so I wouldn't have any."

"He's alive," Tool proclaims. "Shoulder wound, finger missing, bruised up pretty damn good, but he should be okay."

"Watch her." Reaper hands me off to Tongue, giving me a quick kiss before he kneels next to Boomer.

"Can't believe you strung that fucker up like a fish," Tongue notices. "It's impressive. Your fight, your will."

"I did what I had to." I never take my eyes off Reaper as he lifts Boomer into his arms.

"Reaper?" Boomer slurs half-awake. "Reaper? Is that you?"

"It's me, kid. You're going to be alright."

"Sarah," he struggles to say through a broken wheeze. "Sarah…"

"I'm okay! Boomer," I cry and try to run toward him, but Tongue stops me.

"Give them a minute."

"After this, Boomer. Will you please take your prospect cut? Your father's vest has been waiting for you."

"Yeah," Boomer whispers. "I'll take the damn thing."

Tongue picks me up next and throws me over his shoulder. I guess being cradled against someone's chest is a little too intimate. I can't see anything as we walk, just the steps. When we finally get to the door, Tongue climbs up a ladder until the hot desert sun burns my face and eyes.

I lift my hand to block the sun out of my eyes. Shit, it's bright.

"I saw what you did to him," Reaper says after he gets Boomer settled in a truck one of the guys drove. "My little maniac, I'm so fucking glad you're fucked in the head."

"I am not!" I protest, wrapping my arms around his neck.

He chuckles, bringing his forehead to mine.

"Okay, just a little." I place my fingers together to show just how little, and Reaper presses them together more to make the area smaller.

"There. That's better." He places a kiss on my lips, and then I remember that Fabian kissed me. I rip my lips away, unable to meet Reaper's eyes. I'm so disgusted with myself. "What is it? Kiss me, baby. I need your lips. I love you."

"He kissed me," I say. "I pulled away. It made me sick. I—I didn't kiss him back, but he kissed me."

Reaper growls, and the promise of danger and violence shivers over my skin from the sound. He cups my cheek and tilts my head, and then he kisses me again. "It makes me want to kill that fucker all over again. I know anything you did, you had to do to stay alive."

"I didn't kiss him back, Reaper. I would rather die. It made me sick. Literally, I threw up."

"Don't ever say that. I always want you to do what you have to. I want you to come back to me. I hate the thought of a man putting his hands on you, but I trust you to handle yourself until I know I can get to you." He tucks me into his side, and Tool comes up to me and places a grenade in my hand.

"I found it in Boomer's pocket. Want to do the honors?" he asks.

"No." I shake my head. "Boomer should. It was him who saved me this entire time. I'd be dead if it wasn't for him."

Boomer falls out of the truck, and Bullseye helps him back up. I pull out of Reaper's arms and run to my brother, wrapping one arm around his waist. I'm getting a lot of practice at this, carrying men who are way too big for me. "I got it, Bullseye."

Boomer is heavy since he can't really walk, but he has his good arm over my shoulder, grunting with every step we take to the shaft that hid us. He wheezes in my ear, spits blood, a gurgling sound in the back of his throat, and I'm afraid he might not make it home. "This is for you, Boomer." I hand him the grenade. "Thank you for saving my life," I say.

He shakes his head and gives me a bloody kiss on the forehead. "Let's do it together."

"Alright." I pull on the clip, and Boomer tosses the green ball down the shaft.

As fast as I can, I drag us as far away as possible. I lean him against the truck, and I can see he is on the edge of passing out.

"Three, two," he counts down.

"One," I finish.

Boom.

EPILOGUE

Reaper

Six weeks later

I WAKE UP WITH A HOT MOUTH WRAPPED AROUND MY COCK, sucking me down her throat like a professional. Well, it's either a really good dream, or I'm about to have the best morning of my life. I rub the sleep out of my eyes and glance down to see my blonde bombshell staring at me through burning amber eyes as her lips stretch all around me.

"Good morning, doll." My voice is still heavy with sleep.

She mumbles something back, but I can't tell what it is since she has a mouth full of cock. "Mmm, look at you." I wrap her hair around each fist and use them as reins to move her head faster. "Fuck, yes. That's it, Sarah. Take all of my cock. Come on, doll. You can do it." I whisper words of encouragement as I flex my hips and hit the back of her throat. She gags a bit, something that's been happening more often than not.

She didn't use to have a reflex, but after what happened, I think she's more sensitive now. "Sorry, doll, I'll go easier."

I watch as her tongue swirls around me, licking me from root to tip, lapping at the plum crown and sensitive glands. "You are so fucking good at this," I groan, seeing the shine of her spit sparkle on my dick in the morning sun peeking through the curtains.

She's wearing the cut I had made just for her. On the back it says, 'Property of Reaper' with the Ruthless Kings rocker on it. She's the first ol' lady in the club, and I have a feeling now that the guys see how happy I am and how amazing it is to have one woman in your bed, they'll want to settle down too.

She rubs her fingers between my asshole and my sack, pressing against the sensitive skin. It's a spot I had no idea I liked, but when she did it the first time, I lost my load in five seconds. "Don't you dare. I'm not ready to be done with you just yet."

She smiles around my shaft when she knows I figured out her plan to make me come quick. That's not happening. Actually, I prefer it never to happen because quick is just not enough time with my doll.

"You find that funny?" Quick, I wrap my arms around her slim back and flip us so I'm hovering over her. I fuck my cock inside her tight pussy in one stroke. "You're so wet. Does sucking my dick turn you on that much?"

"Yes," she hisses as I fill her up and stretch her out. "I love your cock in my mouth."

That only makes my orgasm inch closer. She's so beautiful and magical. I'm not sure what I deserved to have her in my life. Our road wasn't easy, by any means. Everything and everyone was against us. Hell, I was my own worst enemy.

But fate won, and now I'm the happiest I have ever been in my life.

Her eyes shut, and I watch the variety of expressions cross her face with every stroke I give her. We always go hard. We always fuck. But right now, with how angelic she looks with her golden hair around her, reminding me of a halo, I decide to show her how much I love her.

I rock in and out of her, taking my cock out to the point where the tip is all that's left, and then gently, I slide back in. She cries out, arching her back, and her fingers dig into my back, over my freshly healed scars from the accident.

I kiss down her tan skin, the canvas of a goddess, and suck one of her nipples into my mouth, praising her to show how blessed I am. Her tits are heavier, swollen, and her nipples are redder than usual. I love her tits just how they are, but when they get like this, it's like a treat I don't expect to have.

I lap at them, rolling them between my teeth. She clenches around me when I pop off her tight bead and move to the next one. I play with her mounds, jiggling them and watching them bounce. Something is so different about them. I can't put my finger on it. It isn't that time of the month because she doesn't get this turned on from it.

"Reaper," she whispers.

Mmm, fuck, I love it when she says my road name in bed. "Yeah, doll?"

"Harder."

"No."

"Reaper!" she cries from my protest. "Please!"

"I said no, doll." I pull my cock from her sweet cunt, and she reaches for me, hungry for my dick, but I slap her hand away.

"I can't believe you'd deny a pregnant woman."

She says that right as I wrap my hand around myself to give a solid stroke. "What did you just say?" I stare at her, stunned in disbelief.

She crawls onto her knees and straightens so we are looking one another in the eye. Sarah grabs my hand and places it on her stomach and exhales dreamily. "I'm pregnant, Reaper."

For one moment, my heart stops beating, and I stare at my hand that's lying flat against her stomach. My hand engulfs her. She's so little. "You're pregnant?" I repeat.

She nods. "I found out yesterday. I've been trying to figure out how to tell you."

Something inside me grows, claws, and snaps. She's mine. She really is mine. With a savage snarl, I pick her up and stand, bending her over the bed. I slide my way into her again. It isn't slow. It's hard. I don't know what's wrong with me. It's like I need to mark her again, claim her. I'm not sure. This need, it's feral.

"Reaper!" she screams as I slam inside her. Every stroke is harder than the last. I keep one hand on her hip and the other on her stomach, pounding my filthy way inside her.

I can't contain how happy I am. Finally, after so many years of wondering if I was going to die alone, someone decided I deserve happiness.

I'm snarling, pounding ruthlessly into her sweet cunt. Sweat fills the air, fueling me further. It's like she's pouring gasoline all over me, igniting that fire that is turning into a wild blaze. I can't be controlled. I curl over her when her first orgasm rips through, sucking me deep and begging for my seed, but I don't give it to her.

No.

211

She has it already, greedy girl. And it's growing inside her as we live, as we breathe. I'm not sure what the hell I'm going to do with a baby here at the MC, but it will be the most protected person in this club.

"I love you," I whisper into her ear. "I love you so fucking much, and I'll protect you and our child until my last breath."

"Let me see you," she says.

I flip us again until she is on her back, and I can see her wet lashes. Her tits, it all makes sense, and why the smell of bacon has been making her sick. I drop onto my elbows and slow down again, pressing our mouths together in a passionate kiss. I still, keep my hand flat against her belly, and moan.

"I'm going to come," she says.

"Not yet. With me. Come with me," I beg, quickening my thrusts until the only sounds in the room are our breaths mingling and my sack slapping against her ass. She's dripping wet, scorching, and if she wasn't pregnant before, she will be after today.

In unison, we climax, her pussy squeezing me tight and sucking the seed from my dick. I fill her up, grunting into her mouth, lavishing her soft skin with my hands, touching every part of her. I plant myself so deep that she cries out again when I hit that sensitive spot, and she shatters beneath me again.

She's more sensitive now.

I'm already liking the change in her body. Fuck, my cock swells when I think of her round belly and her wobble as she walks. She'll lay her hand on her stomach, rubbing our baby, comforting him or her. And I want to fuck her all over again now.

She's going to be an amazing mother.

"Wow," she says. She stretches her arms above her head and yawns. "I'm going to take a nap."

I kiss the tip of her nose, inhaling the smell of peaches from her hair, and pull out of her with a grunt. I clean us up and tuck her in. I stare at her. So many things were against us, and here we are, beating the odds. She's already asleep by the time I'm dressed. I slide out the door, and it's on the tip of my tongue to tell everyone, but maybe she wants it to be a surprise, so I keep my mouth shut.

I have a feeling everyone will be happy, maybe even Boomer.

There's one person I need to talk to, though.

I walk by a few cut-sluts, and some of the guys are laughing and playing pool, lifting their beers to me as I walk out the door that Tank fixed for a second time. The early morning sun is bright, and somehow the stars have managed to stay out. I light a cigarette and lean against the porch, staring up at the sky like it has all the answers.

"Hawk, man, I have no idea where to start." I take an inhale of my smoke, nervous, and wondering if I'm crazy for talking to nothing but the everlasting sky. "I know you didn't know about her, but I know you do know. She's strong, like you, like Boomer, and before you go wishing you could kick my ass, know that I love her more than anything in this world. She's safe with me. I'm not asking for your permission because I'm going to love her anyway. She's pregnant. She's perfect. I'm happy and—" I get a bit choked up because I wish he was here so fucking bad. "I wish you were here to see it, to meet your daughter and your grandbaby. I want you to know I have them. I'm going to take care of them. You can trust me. I'll lay my life down. I'll carve out any hearts, my own included. You're missed, old friend. I don't know how life got to be where it's at, but I have no doubt in my mind that she's here because you sent her to me. I'll see you later rather than sooner, I hope." I suck another drag of smoke in my lungs and grin. "She's fucking crazy, just like you. It must run in your damn blood. It's the only thing I worry about with my kid. Let me tell you what she did. She strung up this guy on a hook—" I proceed to tell him about how I found her, beating her captor and being a complete badass.

"She's so damn strong. A little whacked in the head, but I guess she wouldn't be mine if she wasn't, right?" I stare at the sky, the darkness of the night blends with the yellow rays of the sun, and the stars start to disappear.

My only wish is to know he can hear me.

A shooting star bursts across the sky, and I don't believe in shit like that, but right now, I'm going to.

"What are you doing?" Sarah wraps her arms around me and kisses my shoulder.

A few more shooting stars cross the sky. "Just wondering how I'm going to handle not one, but two maniacs. Have you met you?"

"Oh, you better stop!" She slaps my shoulder, and I throw her over my shoulder and slap her ass. She laughs, the sound music to my ears.

I take one last look at the sky, and I swear one of the stars winks at me.

Yeah, I don't believe in much, but maybe now is the time to start. I have fate on my side, love, and the MC. Life is good.

And as long as I have my little maniac, I'll be alright.

ACKNOWLEDGMENTS

Austin—Y'alls blessing means more then you'll ever know.

To my twin yes you the instigator to my bad decisions you rock

H.R. I promise I'll explain later.

Little Girl thanks for everything and putting up with all my whining
*pic

Thanks for all the late-night discussions listening to me work things out in my head.

Silla Webb thanks for swooping in to save this release.

M.J. Seriously you're the greatest always there to talk me of a ledge and point me in the right direction

L.A. You have been there through every milestone for me thanks for being such a fantastic friend

To D.R.—Even though we don't have the same taste in teams, thanks for sharing your better half with me.

ALSO BY K.L. SAVAGE

PREQUEL - REAPER'S RISE
BOOK ONE - REAPER
BOOK TWO - BOOMER
BOOK THREE - TOOL
BOOK FOUR - POODLE
BOOK FIVE - SKIRT
BOOK SIX - PIRATE
BOOK SEVEN - DOC
BOOK EIGHT - TONGUE

OTHER BOOKS IN THE RUTHLESS KINGS SERIES
A RUTHLESS HALLOWEEN

RUTHLESS KINGS MC IS NOW ON AUDIBLE.

CLICK HERE TO JOIN RUTHLESS READERS AND GET
THE LATEST UPDATES BEFORE ANYONE ELSE. OR
VISIT AUTHORKLSAVAGE.COM OR STALK THEM AT
THE SITES BELOW.

FACEBOOK | INSTAGRAM | RUTHLESS READERS
AMAZON | TWITTER | BOOKBUB | GOODREADS |
PINTEREST | WEBSITE

FOR UPDATES FROM
K.L. SAVAGE TEXT:

KL SAVAGE

RUTHLESS ROMANCE THAT WILL *RIP* YOUR HEART OUT.

725-225-0825

Printed in Great Britain
by Amazon

24642488R00126